THE SKATING RINK

THE SKATING RINK

ROBERTO BOLAÑO

Translated by Chris Andrews

PICADOR

First published 2009 by New Directions Books, New York
and simultaneously by Penguin Books Canada

First published in Great Britain 2010 by Picador
an imprint of Pan Macmillan, a division of Macmillan Publishers Limited
Pan Macmillan, 20 New Wharf Road, London N1 9RR
Basingstoke and Oxford
Associated companies throughout the world
www.panmacmillan.com

ISBN 978-0-330-51052-3 HB
ISBN 978-0-330-52305-9 TPB

Originally published in 1993 as *La Pista de Hielo* in Spain;
published by arrangement with the Heirs of Roberto Bolaño and
Carmen Balcells Agencia Literaria, Barcelona.

1 3 5 7 9 8 6 4 2

A CIP catalogue record for this book is available from
the British Library.

Printed in the UK by CPI Mackays, Chatham ME5 8TD

Visit **www.picador.com** to read more about all our books
and to buy them. You will also find features, author interviews and
news of any author events, and you can sign up for e-newsletters
so that you're always first to hear about our new releases.

If I must live then let it be
rudderless, in delirium
Mario Santiago

Remo Morán:

The first time I saw him, it was in the Calle Bucareli

The first time I saw him, it was in the Calle Bucareli, in Mexico City, that is, back in the vague shifty territory of our adolescence, the province of hardened poets, on a night of heavy fog, which slowed the traffic and prompted conversations about that odd phenomenon, so rare in Mexico City at night, at least as far as I can remember. Before he was introduced to me, at the door of the Café La Habana, I heard his deep velvety voice, the one thing that hasn't changed over the years. He said: This is just the night for Jack. He was referring to Jack the Ripper, but his voice seemed to be conjuring lawless territories, where anything was possible. We were adolescents, all of us, but seasoned already, and poets, so we laughed. The stranger's name was Gaspar Heredia, Gasparín to his casual friends and enemies. I can still remember the fog seeping in under the revolving doors and the wisecracks flying back and forth. Faces and lamps barely emerged from the gloom, and, wrapped in that cloak, everyone seemed enthusiastic and ignorant, fragmentary and innocent, as in fact we were. Now we're thousands of miles from the Café La Habana, and the fog is thicker than it was back then, better still for Jack the Ripper. From the Calle Bucareli, in Mexico City, to murder, you must be thinking . . . But it's not like that at all, which is why I'm telling you this story . . .

GASPAR HEREDIA:

I came to Z, from Barcelona, halfway through the spring

I came to Z, from Barcelona, halfway through the spring. I had hardly any money left, but wasn't too worried, because there was a job waiting for me in Z. Remo Morán, who I hadn't seen for many years, although I was always hearing about him, except for a while there when he disappeared off the radar, had offered me a season's work, from May to September; the offer came through a mutual friend. I should point out that I didn't ask for the job; I hadn't been in touch with Morán, and never intended to come and live in Z. It's true we'd been friends, but a long time before, and I'm not the sort to ask for charity. Until then I'd been sharing an apartment with three other people in the Chinese quarter, and things weren't going as badly as you might think. After a few months, my legal situation in Spain became, however, to put it mildly, precarious: without residency or a work permit, I was, and am, living indefinitely in a kind of purgatory until I can scrape up enough money to get out of the country or hire a lawyer to sort out my papers. And of course that's a dream, for a foreigner like me with little or nothing to call his own. But anyway, things weren't going too badly. I had a long series of casual jobs, from manning a newspaper stand on the Ramblas to sewing up leather bags in a sweatshop with a rickety old Singer, and that was how I earned enough to eat, go to the movies and pay for my room. One day I met

Mónica, a Chilean girl who had a stall in the Ramblas; we got talking and it turned out that both of us had been friends with Remo Morán, at different times in our lives: I'd met him years before, while she'd gotten to know him more recently in Europe and seen him pretty often. She told me he was living in Z (I knew he was somewhere in Spain) and said it would be crazy, given my situation, not to visit him or at least give him a call. And ask for help? Naturally I did nothing of the sort. Remo and I had drifted too far apart, and I didn't want to bother him. So I went on living or surviving, it depended, until one day Mónica told me that she'd seen Remo Morán in a bar in Barcelona, and when she'd explained my situation, he'd said I should go straight to Z, where he could find me a place to live and a job for the summer at least. Morán remembered me! I have to admit I didn't have any better offers, and up until then my prospects had been as black as a bucket of motor oil. The idea of it appealed to me too. There was nothing to keep me in Barcelona; I was just getting over the worst flu of my life (I still had a fever when I got to Z), and the mere thought of spending five months by the sea made me smile like an idiot. All I had to do was jump on the train that runs up the coast. No sooner said than done: I filled my backpack with books and clothes, and cleared off. I gave away everything I couldn't carry. As the train drew out of the Estación de Francia, I thought: I'm never living in Barcelona again. Get thee behind me! No regrets! By the time I reached Mataró I had begun to forget the faces I was leaving behind . . . But that's just a figure of speech, of course, you never really forget . . .

ENRIC ROSQUELLES:

Until a few years ago I was a typical mild-mannered guy

Until a few years ago I was a typical mild-mannered guy; ask my family, my friends, my junior colleagues, anyone who came into contact with me. They'll all tell you I'm the last person you'd expect to be involved in a crime. My life is orderly and even rather austere. I don't smoke or drink much; I hardly go out at night. I'm known as a hard worker: if I have to, I can work a sixteen-hour day without flagging. I was awarded my psychology degree at the age of twenty-two, and it would be false modesty not to mention that I was one of the top students in my class. At the moment I'm studying law; in fact, I should have finished the degree already, but I decided to take things easy. I'm in no hurry. To tell you the truth I often think it was a mistake to enroll in law school. Why am I putting myself through this? It's more and more of a drag as the years go by. Which doesn't mean I'm going to give up. I never give up. Sometimes I'm slow and sometimes I'm quick—part tortoise, part Achilles—but I never give up. It has to be admitted, however, that it's not easy to work and study at the same time, and as I was saying, my job is generally intense and demanding. Of course it's my own fault. I'm the one who set the pace. Which makes me wonder, if you'll allow me a digression, why I took on so much in the first place. I don't know. Sometimes things get away from me. Sometimes I think my behavior was inexcusable. But then, other times, I think: I was walking around in a daze, mostly. Lying awake all night, as I have done recently, hasn't helped me find any answers. Nor have the abuse and insults to which I have, apparently, been subjected. All I know for sure is that I took on too much responsibility too soon. For a brief, happy period of my life I worked as a psychologist with a group of maladjusted children. I should have stuck to that, but there are things you can only understand years later, with the benefit of hindsight. And anyway I think it's normal for a young man to want to improve himself, to have ambitions and goals. I did, anyway. That was what brought me to Z, not long after the socialists won the municipal elections for the first time. Pilar needed someone to manage the Social Services Department, and they chose me. My CV wasn't monumental, but there was enough in it to qualify me for the job, which was complicated and, as in many socialist municipalities, almost experimental. Naturally, I'm a paid-up party member (unless, that is, they've already made an example of me by publicly revoking my membership) but that had nothing to do with their final decision: they went through my application with a fine-tooth comb, and those first six months were exhausting, not to mention turbulent. I'd like to take this opportunity to speak out against those who are trying to claim that Pilar was somehow implicated in this shameful affair. She didn't give me the job as a personal favor, although in the course of her two terms in office (say what you like, the citizens of Z love their mayor!) we did, I am proud to say, become friends, companions in hardship and in hope, and, for me, that friendship extended to her husband Enric Gibert i Vilamajó, whose first name I am honored to share. The vultures with press passes can print what they like. If Pilar ever erred, it was in granting me her trust, more and more fully as time went by. If you examine the state of the various departments before my arrival and, say, two years afterward, it's immediately clear that I was the driving force behind the Z city council, its muscles and its brain. It didn't matter how tired I was, I always got on with my work, and often took on the work of others. I also provoked resentment and envy, even within my own team. I know that many of my junior colleagues secretly hated me. Gradually, I became irritable and bitter. I confess that I never imagined spending the rest of my life in Z: a professional should always aspire to greater things. In my case I would have been delighted to undertake a similar job in Barcelona or at least in Gerona. I'm not ashamed to admit that I often dreamed of being summoned by the mayor of a great capital to manage a bold project for the prevention of delinquency or drug abuse. I had already done all I could do in Z. Pilar wasn't going to be mayor forever, and what would become of me when she was gone, what sort of politicians would I have to bow and scrape to? Such were the fears I tried to assuage as I drove home each night. Alone and exhausted each and every night. When I think of all the things I had to do, everything I had to swallow and stomach, all on my own! Until I met Nuria and the plan for the Palacio Benvingut came to me . . .

REMO MORÁN:

It's true: in May I found a job for Gaspar Heredia

It's true: in May I found a job for Gaspar Heredia, Gasparín to his friends, a Mexican, a poet, and flat broke at the time. I'd never have admitted it, but I was in a state of nervous agitation as I anticipated his arrival. And yet when he appeared at the door of the Cartago, I hardly recognized him. The years had taken their toll. We gave each other a hug, and that was it. I often think that if we'd got talking or gone for a walk along the beach, and then drunk a bottle of cognac and broken down crying or laughed until dawn, I'd be telling a different story now. But after we hugged, a mask of ice clamped itself over my face, preventing the slightest expression of friendship. I knew he was helpless, small and alone, perched on his stool at the bar, but I did nothing. Was I ashamed? Had his presence in Z released some kind of monster? I don't know. Maybe I thought I'd seen a ghost, and in those days I found ghosts extremely unpleasant. Not any more. Now, on the contrary, they brighten up my afternoons. It was after midnight when we left the Cartago, and I couldn't even bring myself to try to make conversation. Still, although he was silent too, I sensed he was happy. At the campground's office, El Carajillo ("coffee with a dash"), as he was known, had the television on and didn't notice us. We kept on going. The tent that was to be Gaspar's home had been pitched off to one side, next to the tool shed. It had to be in a relatively quiet place, since he would be sleeping during the day. Gasparín was perfectly content; in his deep voice he said it would be like living out in the country. As far as I know, he's lived in cities all his life. On one side of the tent there was a tiny pine, more like a Christmas tree than the sort of pine you normally find in a campground. (Because the spot had been chosen by Alex, and he was always playing some incomprehensible mind game, I couldn't help trying to guess at its arcane significance. Was Gasparín like a Christmas present?) After that I took him to the washrooms and showed him how the showers worked, and then we went back to reception. That was it. I didn't see him again until a week later, or something like that. Gasparín and El Carajillo became good friends. It's hard not to be friends with El Carajillo. Gasparín worked the standard hours for a night watchman, from ten at night till eight in the morning. Night watchmen sleep on the job, that's par for the course. The pay was good, better than the other campgrounds, and there wasn't too much work, although Gasparín had to do most of it. El Carajillo is very old and almost always too drunk to go out and do the rounds at four in the morning. Meals were provided by the company: that is, me. Gasparín could have breakfast, lunch and dinner at the Cartago, and he didn't have to pay a peseta. Sometimes I checked with the waiters: Did the night watchman come for lunch? Does he usually have dinner here? How long since he's been in? And sometimes, though less often, I would ask: Have you seen him writing? Scribbling in the margins of a book? Or staring at the moon like a wolf? I didn't persist, though, mainly because I didn't have time. . . . Or rather, I was busy with things that had nothing to do with the distant shrunken figure of Gaspar Heredia, who seemed to be turning his back on the world, giving nothing away, hiding who he was and what he was made of, and the courage it had taken to keep on walking (or running, more like it!) toward the darkness, toward the heights . . .

GASPAR HEREDIA:

The campground was called Stella Maris

The campground was called Stella Maris (a name reminiscent of rooming houses) and it was a place where there weren't too many rules, or too many fights and robberies. It was frequented by working-class families from Barcelona and young people of modest means from France, Holland, Italy and Germany. The combination was sometimes explosive and would have blown up in my face for sure if I hadn't immediately adopted El Carajillo's golden rule, which consisted basically of letting them kill each other. His harsh way of putting it, which struck me as funny at first, then disturbing, didn't reflect a contemptuous attitude to the clients; on the contrary, it sprang from a profound respect for their right of self-determination. El Carajillo was popular, as I soon found out, especially with the Spaniards and various foreign families who came back to Z year after year for their summer holidays. In the course of his one, protracted round of the campground, he was continually invited into campers and tents, where he was always offered something to help him while away the night: a drink, a slice of cake or a porn magazine. As if he needed any help! By three in the morning the old man was drunk as a skunk and you could hear him snoring from the street. Round about then, calm descended on the tents, and it was pleasant to walk down the campground's narrow graveled alleys, with my flashlight switched off and nothing to do but listen to the sound of my own footsteps. Before setting off on my round I'd sit on the wooden bench by the main gate talking with El Carajillo while the sleepless and the revelers went in and out bidding us good night. Sometimes we had to carry a drunk to his tent. El Carajillo led the way because he always knew where each person was camped, and I followed with the client on my back. Occasionally we got tips for this and other services, but usually we weren't even thanked. At first I tried to stay awake all night. Then I followed El Carajillo's example. We retired to the office, switched off the lights and settled down, each in a leather armchair. The office was a prefabricated box with two glass walls, one facing the entrance, the other facing the swimming pool, so it was easy to keep a more or less effective watch from inside. The power for the whole campground often failed, and I was the one who had to go into the Outer Darkness and solve the problem; not that it was really dangerous, but in the little hut where the fuses were, you had to squeeze past a whole lot of dangling wires. There were also spiders and all sorts of insects. The buzz of electricity! The campers, whose television viewing had been interrupted by the blackout, applauded when the lights came back on. Occasionally, but not very often, the *guardia civil* came by. El Carajillo dealt with them; he laughed at their jokes, and invited them in, but they never got out of the car. Apparently, they could drink for free at the Stella Maris bar, but I never saw them there. Occasionally the police would put in an appearance. The national or the town police. Routine visits. They didn't even acknowledge my presence, which was just as well. And when they turned up I often found a pretext to go and do a round of the campground. I remember one night the *guardia civil* came looking for two women from Zaragoza who had arrived that day. We said they weren't there. When they had gone, El Carajillo looked at me and said: Let the poor girls sleep in peace. It was all the same to me. The next night El Carajillo warned them and they cleared out as fast as they could. I didn't ask for explanations. Each morning, as day was breaking, I would go the beach. It's the best time: the sand is clean, as if freshly combed, and there are no tourists, just fishing boats pulling in their nets. I'd take off my clothes, go for a swim and return to the campground, picking my way through the reeds. By the time I got back to reception, El Carajillo had usually woken up and opened the windows to air the office. We'd sit down on the bench out front, raise the entrance barrier, and talk, usually about the weather. Cloudy, sultry, mild, breezy, overcast, rainy, sunny, hot . . . For some reason that I never discovered, El Carajillo was obsessed with the weather. Not at night, though. At night his favorite topic was war, specifically the final years of the Spanish Civil War. The story was always the same, with minor variations: a group of Republican soldiers, armed with hand grenades, was advancing toward a tank formation. The tanks opened fire; the soldiers flattened themselves on the ground, and after a few moments began to advance again. Again the tanks sprayed the squad with machine-gun fire, the soldiers dropped to the ground, and then resumed their advance; after the fourth or fifth repetition there was a new and terrifying development: the tanks, which had been standing still until then, began to move toward the soldiers. Two out of three times he told the story, El Carajillo's face went red at this point, as if he was suffocating, and he began to cry. What happened then? Some soldiers turned and ran, others kept going toward the tanks, and most of them were cut down screaming and cursing. Sometimes, if the story lasted a bit longer, I got a glimpse of one or two tanks burning amidst the dead bodies and the chaos. Shit-scared, on they went. Shit-scared, who needs legs? It was never clear which side El Carajillo had fought on, and I never asked him. Maybe it was all made up; there weren't many tanks in the Spanish Civil War. In Barcelona I met an old butcher in the Boquería market who swore he had been in a trench less than two yards away from Marshall Tito. He wasn't a liar, but as far as I know Tito was never in Spain. So how the hell did he turn up in the butcher's memory? A mystery. After drying his tears, El Carajillo went on drinking as if nothing had happened, or proposed a game of three coin. With a bit of practice I became an expert. Three of yours, three with what you're holding, two and one of yours makes three, one and what you're holding makes three, my three, your three, and the one-eyed man has three as well; three, all done! There were always some night owls among the campers who'd come and join in, city folk from Barcelona who couldn't sleep because of the silence, or older guys who were spending the summer months with their children's families. El Carajillo's friends. Sometimes, when I got tired of the office, I'd hang out in the bar. That was a different scene altogether, like a gathering of George Romero's living dead. Between one and two in the morning the barman would lock up and switch off the lights. Before driving away, he'd ask that all the bottles and glasses be left on a designated table on the terrace. No one ever paid any attention. The last to leave were usually two women. Or rather, an old woman and a girl. One talked and laughed as if her life depended on it, while the other listened absently. Both of them seemed ill . . .

ENRIC ROSQUELLES:

I know that whatever I say will only make things worse

I know that whatever I say will only make things worse; but still, let me tell it my way. I am not a monster, or the cynical unscrupulous character that you have been portraying in such lurid colors. Perhaps you find my physical appearance amusing. Go ahead and laugh. There was a time when people trembled before me. I'm fat, five foot eight, and Catalan. Also, I'm a socialist and I believe in the future. Or used to. Forgive me. I'm going through something of a rough patch. I believed in hard work, justice and progress. I know that Pilar used to boast about having me as her right-hand man when she met with the other socialist mayors in the province. Well, I always supposed she did, although now, in my new-found solitude, I keep wondering why I was never headhunted, why some big shot never tried to snatch me away from Z and Pilar, and give me a job somewhere closer to Barcelona. Maybe Pilar didn't boast enough. Maybe they all had their own indispensable helpers and didn't need anyone else. Within the bounds of Z, my power grew. And that sealed my fate. Z was where I did my good works as well as the deeds for which I shall have to pay. Although the Z City Council reviles me now, it still depends on all the projects and studies I supervised. I was the head of the Social Services Department, as I said, but I also looked after Urban Planning, and even the head of Parks and Recreation, a child molester who has the nerve to insult me now, used to come into my office each morning and ask for my advice. At festivities and official functions, I was always at Pilar's side. Don't jump to conclusions: for some reason, I don't know why, our mayor's husband hated gatherings of more than six people. Enric Gibert is what you might call an intellectual. Perhaps I would have been better off staying busy in my office like him, God only knows, but I didn't and that was how I met Nuria, at an official function in the Z Sporting Complex . . . Nuria Martí . . . When I think of that afternoon, I can't hold back the tears . . . We were rather arbitrarily rewarding the merits of Z's outstanding athletes. The prizewinners included a junior basketball team, which had done very well that season; a young soccer player who was in a second division A team; the trainer of Z's football club, which was in the fourth division (he was retiring that year); the young waterpolo players who had won the league championship; and finally, the star, Nuria Martí, who had just come back from Copenhagen, where she had defended the national colors, no less, in a figure-skating competition. . . . The pavilion was full of primary school students (their teachers had brought them for an outing) and when Nuria appeared in person the place went crazy. They were all shouting and clapping! Little ten-year-old squirts whistling and shouting *Hurray for Nuria!* I've never seen anything like it. Not that there had been some sudden figure-skating craze; it's a sport with a small following, as everybody knows. Some of the kids, the girls especially, had watched the event on television and of course they had seen Nuria skate. For a few of them, she was an idol. But most of them were simply responding to the magnetic force of her fame and beauty. There, in front of me, was the most beautiful woman I had ever seen. The most beautiful woman I will ever see! They say children are good judges of character. As a psychologist and civil servant, I've never been convinced. But at least that time they were right. All the world's adjectives fell short of Nuria's luminous form. How could I have worked for so many years in Z without meeting her? The only explanation I can find is that I didn't actually live in Z, and up until then, Nuria had spent long periods away, on a grant from the Spanish Olympic Committee. During the days that followed this sublime apparition (I'm afraid I can't describe it any other way), I kept searching, almost unconsciously, for a pretext that would allow me, if not to become friends with Nuria, at least to say hello to her when we met in the street, and perhaps chat for a while. To that end, I invented a new title: Queen of the Annual Fair of Dairy Products and Vegetables, to be awarded by the Department of Fairs and Festivals, an idea which initially bewildered the committee of exhibiting farmers, but was adopted enthusiastically after a little explanation. I went on to suggest that no one was better suited to be Queen of the Fair than our international skating star, Nuria. A purely ceremonial and symbolic role. She would only have to say a few words at the opening. They were all delighted, so I moved straight on to the hard part of the plan: using that pretext to get her to see me, to recognize me. . . . Needless to say, the fair itself didn't matter to me in the least; for the first time ever my heart was overruling my head, and I was more than happy to follow it. It was spring, I think, and I was constantly aware that I was heading for a fall, a ruinous fall, but I didn't care. I only mention that now so as not to give the false impression that I was blinded. The Coordinator of Fairs and Festivals officially offered her the crown, which, as I had foreseen, she declined. One reason, the Coordinator informed me, was that she would soon be resuming her place on the Spanish skating team. There was clearly no time to lose. I had a valid reason for getting in touch with her, so I called her the same day and we arranged to meet at a place in the historic center of Z. I wasn't able to convince her to accept the title of queen, of course, nor was that my aim, but I did manage to persuade her, in the end, to have dinner with me that week. That was how it all began. I never found out if there was a queen that spring. Our first dinner was followed by others, in rapid succession. I started getting to know the people she mixed with, and gradually my social habits changed. Our chance encounters became increasingly frequent. And increasingly pleasant. I must admit that I would have been content to go on like that for the rest of my life, but nothing lasts forever. As we got to know each other better, I began to get a clearer sense of Nuria's problems; viewed from a different point of view, they might not have been problems at all, but her artistic temperament could quickly blow things out of proportion. I won't mention the hundreds of little obstacles that life began to put in her way at that time. I'll only recount the two that seemed most significant to me. I learned of the first after a pleasant dinner one night in the company of good friends, some of whom now seem to enjoy spitting in my face. When we left, Nuria instructed me to drive out to the coves instead of going straight back to her place. When we got to the farthest one, the cove of San Belisario, she started talking in a hesitant, incoherent way about an affair with some young man about town whom I had not met. I deduced that they had been engaged, and that the engagement had been broken off. I could tell that she was in pain and shock. Luckily it was dark in the car; otherwise she would have seen the contorted expressions on my face, betraying profound disbelief and disgust: how could there be a man capable of leaving her? I can say, however, that by unburdening herself in this way, she took our friendship to a new level of intimacy. How did I try to console her? What words did I find? Forget him. I told her over and over again to forget him and devote herself body and soul to her art, to skating. But, as it happened, the second problem was related to skating. It arose about ten days after Nuria left Z. The Spanish team had gathered in Jaca, in a special training center still under construction, from which Nuria called me at midnight, in floods of tears. They had cut off her grant! The bastards had all got together in Jaca and proceeded to hand out, renew and cut off grants. Nuria was certainly not the only one ambushed like that: in the space of a few hours, one Hungarian and two Scandinavian trainers were fired, not to mention various Spanish trainers, and almost all the skaters over nineteen lost their grants. The exceptions, according to Nuria, were highly suspicious. The story appeared the following day, not splashed on the cover of sports magazines, but tucked inside, in a single column of the winter sports section, and never made it into the national newspapers. For Nuria, however, it was a terrible blow. The Spanish Skating Federation had decided it had to rejuvenate itself or die, not an uncommon policy in Spain and generally quite futile. We all have to die a bit every now and then and usually it's so gradual that we end up more alive than ever. Infinitely old and infinitely alive. As for Nuria, she was removed from the national team, but not from the Catalonian Federation, whose facilities she could continue to use for training and competitions. She was, understandably, demoralized and wounded in her sporting pride. Although there was, of course, no place for her on the new figure-skating team, she was better, as she said, than the two girls who now shared top billing. From the newspapers and from phone conversations with some journalist friends in Gerona, I was soon able to verify that most of the Catalan skaters had received the same treatment. Was it a case of Castilian, centralist favoritism? I don't know, nor do I care—and at that point in my life all that mattered to me was what made Nuria happy or unhappy. The new situation was in a sense advantageous to me, because without a grant, Nuria would have to live a settled life in Z. But love is not selfish, as I have recently come to realize, and Nuria's feeling of emptiness, the trouble she had adapting to a life without travel, just two weekly train trips to the Barcelona skating rink, made my heart bleed. When she came back to Z we had various conversations, sometimes in my office during working hours (she was the only person who was allowed to interrupt me whenever she liked, apart from Pilar, of course), sometimes down at the fishing port, leaning against the old boats nobody used any more, which smelt, oddly, of face cream, and we always came back to the same topics: the nepotism of the Olympic bureaucrats, the injustice she had suffered, her talent, which would wither away as the months went by. You might be wondering how we could have gone on talking about what was, in the scheme of things, a minor incident, when there were so many important and perhaps even pleasant things we could have said to one another. But Nuria was obsessive like that; when she came across something she didn't understand, she beat her little blonde head against it over and over until she started bleeding. I had already learned that it was best to listen quietly, unless I had a practical solution to propose, but how could I take on the imperious Figure Skating Federation? I couldn't, obviously. All I could do was let time go by. And meanwhile savor our moments together—I could now look forward to some each day—contemplate Nuria, enjoy that perfect weather in Z, and be happy. Did I try to make a move in all that time? Not once. I don't know if it was lack of nerve, fear of spoiling our friendship, laziness or timidity, but I felt it would be prudent to let a little more time elapse. We are the authors of our own misfortunes, I've heard it said, but that fact is I was happy to play the role of the perfect *chevalier servant*. We went to the movies or to bars. We went driving. Sometimes we had dinner at her house, with her mother and her little ten-year-old sister Laia, who treated me, like I'm not sure what, a fiancé, or a future fiancé, I guess, I never really understood, but always in a friendly and relaxed way, in any case. After dinner we'd watch a video, usually one I had brought, or they left us alone in the little lounge, leafing through Nuria's album of press cuttings and photos. Pleasant evenings. I have often thought that I should have stopped there, I should have said: This is enough, I'm happy, what more could I ask for? But love has no time for reasoning or limits, and it pushed me on. And that was how the Palacio Benvingut project began, ineluctably, to take shape . . .

REMO MORÁN:

It's too late to put things right now, and it would be futile to try

It's too late to put things right now, and it would be futile to try; I only want to clarify my part in the events that took place last summer in Z. Don't ask me to be measured and objective; this is my town after all, and although I might have to move on, I don't want to leave under a cloud of deceit and misapprehension. I am not a front man for some Colombian drug lord, contrary to certain rumors. I do not belong to a Latin American mafia gang specializing in the white slave trade. I have absolutely no links to Brazilian bondage and discipline circles, although I have to say I wouldn't mind that. I'm just a man who's had some lucky breaks and a writer, or rather I was. I came to this town years ago, at a dull and dingy time in my life. There's no point going back over it. I had worked as a street vendor in Lourdes, Pamplona, Zaragoza and Barcelona, and saved up a little money. I could have ended up anywhere; by chance I settled in Z. With my savings I rented a place that I turned into a jewelry store; it was the cheapest place I could find but it cost me all I had, down to the last peseta. I soon realized that because of my constant trips to Barcelona in search of stock, which I was buying in absurdly small quantities, it was going to be impossible to run the business without help, so I had to look for an assistant. On one of my trips I met Alex Bobadilla. I was coming back in the train with four thousand pesetas' worth of jewelry and he was dreamily immersed in *The Globetrotter's Guide*. Beside him, on the empty seat, was a little, well-worn backpack, from which a voluminous bag of peanuts was protruding. Alex was sitting there eating and reading; he looked like a Buddhist monk who had decided to become a boy scout, or vice versa; he also looked like a monkey. After observing him attentively, I asked if he was going abroad. He replied that he was planning to, after the summer, in September or October, but first he had to find a job. I offered him one on the spot. That was the beginning of our friendship and our ascent in the world of business. For the first year, Alex and I slept in the store, next to the tables on which we displayed necklaces and pendants during the day. By the end of the season, in September, I had made a healthy profit. I could have kept the money, found a decent apartment or left Z, but instead I leased a bar that had gone bust for some mysterious reason. The Cartago, it's called. I closed the shop and worked in the bar through the winter. Alex stayed with me; he only went away for a weekend to see his parents, a likeable pair of retirees who keep themselves busy tending their garden in Badalona and come to Z once a month, as a rule. They seem more like his grandparents than his parents, really. That winter we made the shop our home; we moved our sleeping bags and foam mats in there, along with our clothes and our books (although I never saw Alex read anything other than *The Globetrotter's Guide*). The Cartago kept us going, and by the following summer we were running two businesses. The jewelry store, which was now well established, made money, but not nearly as much as the bar. Everyone wanted to make the most of their fortnight or week of happiness, as if the Third World War was about to begin. At the end of the season I leased another jewelry store, in Y this time, just a few miles from Z, and I got married too, but I'll tell you about that later. The next season lived up to expectations, and I was able to get a foothold in X, which is south of Y, but close enough to Z for Alex to check on the takings each day. Three seasons later I was already divorced, and as well as the bar and the stores, I had a campground, a hotel and two other places selling jewelry as well as souvenirs and suntan lotion, all doing a roaring trade. The hotel, which was small but comfortable, was called Hotel Del Mar. The campground is Stella Maris. And the shops: Frutos de Temporada, Sol Naciente, Bucanero, Costa Brava and Montané y hijos. Naturally, I haven't changed the names. The Hotel Del Mar belongs to a German widow. The Stella Maris campground is owned by a family of local worthies, who did, at one time, try to run it, which was a complete disaster, so they decided to lease it instead; in fact they would like to sell the land, but no one's prepared to buy it, because you can't build there. One day, no doubt, all the campgrounds in Z will be rezoned and turned into hotels and apartment buildings; then I'll have to choose between buying and pulling out. If I'm still here, that is; I'll probably be long gone. My first store, as its name suggests, used to sell fruit and vegetables. I can't say much about the others: Montané y hijos is the one with the most mysterious past. Who are or were Mr. Montané and his sons? What did they do? The property is leased through an agency, but as far as I know the owner isn't called Montané. Occasionally, to pass the time, I speculate about it, telling Alex it must have been a funeral parlor, an antique store or a place that sold hunting equipment, three kinds of commerce that my assistant finds deeply revolting. They're not ethical, he says. They bring bad luck. Maybe he's right. If Montané & Sons was a hunting store, that might be where I picked up the bad luck, because I haven't always been unlucky . . . Blood . . . Murder . . . The victim's fear . . . I remember a poem, from way back . . . The killer is asleep and the victim is taking pictures of him . . . Did I read that in some book, or write it myself . . . ? I honestly can't remember, although I think I must have written it, in Mexico City, when I used to hang out with the hardened poets, and Gasparín would turn up in the bars of Colonia Guerrero or the Calle Bucareli, after walking right across the city, looking for something, but for what? Or who? Gasparín's black eyes lost in the Mexican fog: why is it that when I think of him the landscape takes on prehistoric forms? Huge and ponderous, emerging from the murk . . . But maybe I didn't write that poem . . . The sleeping killer photographed by the victim, what do you think? In the ideal setting for a crime, the Palacio Benvingut, naturally . . .

GASPAR HEREDIA:

Sometimes, when I looked out through the campground fence

Sometimes, when I looked out through the campground
fence, in the early hours of the morning, I saw him come
out of the disco opposite, drunk and alone, or with people
I didn't know, and neither did he, to judge from his manner: off in a world of his own, like an astronaut or a cast-
away. Once I saw him with a blonde and that was the only
time he seemed happy; the blonde was pretty and the pair
of them seemed to be the last to leave the disco. On the rare
occasions when he saw me, we greeted each other with a
wave, and that was all. The street is broad and at that hour
of the night it often has an eerie feel: the sidewalks are covered with bits of paper, food scraps, empty cans and broken
glass. From time to time, you come across drunks wandering back to their respective hotels and campgrounds; most
of them get lost and end up sleeping on the beach. Once
Remo crossed the street and asked me if the job was going
OK. I said yes and we wished each other good night. We
didn't talk much in general; he hardly ever came to the
campground. Bobadilla would turn up every afternoon,
though, and hang around for a while looking at the books
and the files. I never got to know Bobadilla well; he paid
me each fortnight, but our relations never went further
than that, although they were always polite. Remo was well
liked by the campground staff, and Bobadilla too, though
not as much; they paid well, and if a real problem came up,

they were understanding. For the receptionists, a girl from Z and a Peruvian, who was also the campground's electrician, and the three cleaning ladies, one of whom was from Senegal (her Spanish was limited to *hola* and *adiós*), it was laid-back as workplaces go, and even conducive to romance: the receptionists had fallen in love. In any case, there were very few problems with the employers, and none at all among the employees. That harmony was probably due in part to the atypical composition of the staff: three foreigners without work permits and three old Spaniards no one else would have taken on, that was about it. I don't know if Remo staffed his other businesses like that; I guess not. Miriam, the Senegalese woman, was the only one of the cleaners who didn't live on the site. The other two, Rosa and Azucena, who came from the outskirts of Barcelona, slept in a two-room family tent, next to the main shower block. They were widowed sisters, and topped up their wages with cleaning jobs for an agency that rented out apartments. That was their first year at Stella Maris; the year before they had worked for another campground in Z, which had fired them because, with the various jobs they were doing, they couldn't be relied on to be there when something urgent came up. Although they both worked an average of fifteen hours a day, they still found time to have a few drinks at night, by the light of a butane lamp, sitting on plastic chairs by the front door of their tent, brushing away the mosquitoes and chatting about this and that. Mainly about how filthy human beings are. Their nightly debriefings always came around to shit, in its various forms, as if it was a language they were struggling to decipher. Talking with them I learned that people shat in the showers, on the floors, on either side of the toilet bowl, and even on its edges, which is no mean feat, requiring a considerable degree of balance and skill. People used shit to write on the doors and to foul the hand basins. Shit that had to be shat and then shifted to symbolic and prominent places: the mirror, the fire extinguisher, the faucets. Shit gathered and daubed to make animal forms (giraffes, elephants, Mickey Mouse), or the letters of soccer graffiti, or bodily organs (eyes, hearts, dicks). For the sisters, the supreme offense was that it happened in the women's bathroom too, though not as often, and always with certain tell-tale features suggesting that a single culprit was responsible for those outrages. A "filthy delinquent" they were determined to hunt down. So they joined forces with Miriam and mounted a discreet stake-out, based on the dull and stubborn process of elimination. That is, they kept a close eye on who was using the bathroom, and went in straight after to check on the state of the place. That was how they found out that the fecal disgraces occurred at a certain time of night, and the principal suspect turned out to be one of the two women I used see on the terrace of the bar. Rosa and Azucena complained to the receptionists and spoke to El Carajillo, who told me, and asked if I might have a word with the woman in question, politely, without offending her, just to see what I could do. Not a simple mission, as I'm sure you'll understand. That night I waited on the terrace until everyone had gone. As usual, the two women were the last to leave; they were sitting on the far side, opposite my table, half hidden, under an enormous tree, whose roots had broken up the cement. What are those trees called? Plane trees? Stone pines? I don't know. I went over to the woman with a glass in one hand and my watchman's flashlight in the other. I got within a yard of their table before they showed any sign of having noticed my presence. I asked if I could sit down with them. The old woman chuckled and said, Of course, be our guest, cutie-locks. Both of them had clean hands. Both seemed to be enjoying the cool of the night. I don't know what I came out with. Some nonsense. They were enveloped and protected by a curious air of dignity. The young woman was silent and plunged in darkness. But the old woman was up for a chat, and she was the color of the flaking, crumbling moon. What did we talk about that first time? I can't remember. Even a minute after leaving them, I wouldn't have been able to remember. All I can recall, but these two things I do recall with the utmost clarity, are the old woman's laughter and the young woman's flat eyes. Flat: as if she was looking inwards? Maybe. As if she was giving her eyes a rest? Maybe. Maybe. And meanwhile the old woman kept talking and smiling, speaking enigmatically, as if in code, as if everything there, the trees, the irregular surface of the terrace, the vacant tables, the shifting reflections on the bar's glass canopy, were being progressively erased, unbeknownst to everyone but them. A woman like that, I thought, couldn't have done what she was accused of doing, or if it was her, she must have had her reasons. Above us, on the branches, among the jittery leaves, the campground rats were carrying out their nocturnal maneuvers. (Rats, not squirrels as I had thought the first night!) The old woman began to sing, neither loudly nor softly, as if her voice, attentive to my presence, was also warily climbing down out of the branches. A trained voice. Although I know nothing about opera, I thought I recognized snatches of various arias. But the most remarkable thing was the way she kept switching from language to language, deftly linking little fragments, melodic flourishes produced for my pleasure alone. And I say my pleasure alone because the girl seemed far away the whole time. Occasionally she touched her eyes with the tips of her fingers, but that was all. Although she was clearly not well, she held off coughing with remarkable willpower until the old woman had finished her trills. Did we look each other in the eye at any point? I don't think so, although we might have. And when I looked at her I could tell that her face was working like an eraser. It was coming and going! Even the campground lights began to waver, brightening and fading as I looked at her face and looked away, or perhaps keeping time with the rise and fall of the singer's voice. For a moment I felt something like rapture: the shadows lengthened, the tents swelled like tumors unable to detach themselves from the gravel, the metallic gleaming of the cars hardened into sheer pain. In the distance, at a corner near the entrance gate, I saw El Carajillo. He looked like a statue and I knew he had been observing us for some time. The old woman said something in German and stopped singing. What did you think, cutie-locks? Very nice, I said, and got up. The girl kept staring at her glass. I would have liked to buy them a drink or something to eat, but the bar had been closed for a long time. I wished them good night and left. By the time I got to the corner, El Carajillo was gone. I found him sitting in the office. He had switched on the television. With an air of indifference, he asked me what had happened. I said I didn't think that woman could be the shitter Rosa and Azucena were looking for. I remember what was on television: a replay of a golf tournament in Japan. El Carajillo looked at me sadly and said that it was her, but it didn't matter. What were we going to tell the cleaning ladies? We'd tell them we were working on it, there were other suspects, other angles to consider . . . We'd come up with something . . .

ENRIC ROSQUELLES:

Benvingut emigrated at the end of the nineteenth century, so they say

Benvingut emigrated at the end of the nineteenth century, so they say, then came back after the First World War, and built his palace on the outskirts of town, at the base of the cliff, in the cove now known as Benvingut Cove. There's a street named after him in the old part of town: Carrer Joan Benvingut. And the eminent Catalan's memory is also honored by a bakery, a florist's, a basketwork store and a few old, damp apartments. What did Benvingut do for Z? Well, he came back, and served as an example: he showed that a local boy could make good in the Americas. I should point out straight away that I have little time for heroes of his sort. I admire hard-working people who don't flaunt their wealth, people who strive to modernize the land of their birth and satisfy its needs in spite of all the obstacles that seem to bar the way. But as far as I know, Benvingut was nothing like that. The barely educated son of a fisherman, he came back as Z's Mister Big, one of the richest men in the province. Naturally he was the first to own a car. He was also the first to have a private pool and sauna. The palace was partly designed by a famous architect of the time, López i Porta, one of Gaudí's epigones, and partly by Benvingut himself, which explains the labyrinthine, chaotic, indecisive layout of every storey in the building. And how many stories are there? Not many people know for sure. Viewed from the sea, there seem to be two, and the palace looks as if it were sinking, as if it were built on shifting sands and not on solid rock. Seeing the building from the main entrance, or from the path through the grounds, a visitor would swear there are three stories. In fact there are four. The illusion is created by the arrangement of the windows and the slope of the land. From the sea, the third and fourth stories are visible. From the entrance, the first, the second and the fourth. Oh, the pleasant afternoons I spent there with Nuria, when my plans for the Palacio Benvingut were still simply plans, still possibilities filling my spirit with the poetry and devotion that seemed, at the time, synonymous with love. Oh, the joy of wandering from room to room, opening shutters and wardrobes, discovering quiet interior courtyards and stone statues hidden by weeds! And then, at the end of the tour, when we were tired, it was so lovely to sit by the sea and polish off the sandwiches that Nuria had brought. (A can of beer for me and a bottle of mineral water for her!) Lying awake at night of late, I have often wondered what prompted me to take her to the Palacio Benvingut for the first time. As well as love—whose attempts to please generally come to grief—*The Blue Lagoon* is to blame. Yes, I'm referring to the film, that old movie starring Brooke Shields. To be thoroughly honest, and to indulge your curiosity, I should disclose that the whole Martí family loved *The Blue Lagoon*: Nuria, her mother and her sister Laia simply couldn't get enough of Brooke and Nick's adventures in Paradise. Have you seen *The Blue Lagoon*? Even after sitting through the video five times, in the little lounge of Nuria's apartment, I couldn't find any cinematic merit in it. The joy it gave me initially, not the movie itself but the sight of Nuria's profile as she watched those teenagers in the wild, was gradually replaced by anxiety and fear as we wore out the videotape. Nuria wanted to live on Brooke's island, at least while she was watching that damned film! With her angelic beauty and her perfect, athletic body, she was ideally suited to the change of scene, and would not have suffered by comparison with Brooke. I was the one who was going to suffer, if we persisted with the extrapolation. If Nuria deserved to live on that island, she also deserved a slim, strong, handsome, not to mention young companion, like the boy in the film. The only member of the cast to whom I could claim any resemblance was, sad to say, Peter Ustinov. (Referring to Ustinov, Laia once said that he was a good fat guy although he seemed like a bad fat guy. I felt the remark was meant for me. I blushed.) How could my fatness, my charmless rotundity, bear comparison with Nick's hard biceps? How could my lower-than-average height match the blond's six-foot-plus stature? The mere thought was, objectively, ridiculous. Anyone else would have turned that anxiety into a joke. But I suffered as never before. Clothes and the mirror became benign or malevolent deities. I started trying to run in the mornings and do weights at the gym; I went on diets. People at work began to notice something odd about me, as if I were getting younger. I have excellent teeth! I still have all my hair! I said to myself in front of the mirror: the sort of consolation an analyst might offer. I have an impressive salary! A promising career! But I would have given it all to be with Nuria and to be like Nick. Then it struck me that the Palacio Benvingut was an island of a sort, and I took Nuria there. I took her to my island. A large part of the façade is covered with blue tiles and so are the two towers that rise from the annexes. Navy blue at the bottom and sky blue at the top of both towers. When the sun shines on them, people driving by glimpse a blue flash, a blue staircase climbing the hills. First we observed the shining palace from the car, on a bend in the road, then I invited her in. How did I come to have the keys? Simple: the palace had belonged to the Z city council for years. Nervously, I asked Nuria what she thought. She thought it was fabulous, all of it, fabulous. As pretty as Brooke Shields' island? Much, much prettier! I thought I was going to faint. Nuria danced up and down the salon, saluted the statues and couldn't stop laughing. We extended our tour of the building and soon discovered the gigantic shed housing Joan Benvingut's legendary swimming pool. Covered with filth like a tramp, the swimming pool, which had once been white, seemed to recognize and greet me. Struck dumb, unable to break the spell, I stood there while Nuria ran off through other rooms. I couldn't breathe. The project was born, I would say, there and then, at least in essence, although I always knew I would be found out in the end . . .

Remo Morán:

I met Lola in peculiar circumstances

I met Lola in peculiar circumstances, during my first winter in Z. Someone, some wicked or civic-minded soul, had been in touch with the town's Social Services Department, and one luminous midday she turned up in front of the closed store. She could see me through the window. Like every morning, I was sitting on the floor reading, and her face on the other side of the glass looked calm and superb like a sunspot. If I'd known that she'd come in her capacity as a social worker, she probably wouldn't have seemed so beautiful. But I only found out after getting up to open the door and telling her that the store would be closed until May. With a smile that I will never forget, she said she didn't want to buy anything. Her visit had been prompted by a complaint. The picture, as it had been painted, was more or less like this: a boy called Alex, who wasn't going to school; his older brother or his father (me), who seemed to have no gainful employment and just sat reading in the front of the store when the sun warmed it up—a suspicious pair of South Americans who seemed to be turning a business in the middle of the tourist district into an unfit dwelling. Whatever the reasons for making the complaint, the source of this information must have been as good as blind. I took Lola straight across to the Cartago, which was empty apart from Alex, who was running through a list of Istanbul's bottom-end options for the hundredth time.

After the introductions, we offered her a glass of cognac; then Alex got out his papers and proved that he was no longer a minor. Lola started saying that she was very sorry, people often make mistakes like that. I asked her to come back to the store, so she could see that there was nothing insalubrious about it. And while I was at it, I showed her my books, told her about my favorite Catalan poet and the Spanish poets I admired, the same old spiel. But she still couldn't understand why we lived in the store and not in an apartment or a rooming house. That incident taught me several things: first, that South Americans are regarded with a certain degree of suspicion; second, that the Z city council doesn't like retailers sleeping on the floor of their business premises; and third, that Alex was taking on my accent, which was disturbing. At the time Lola was twenty-two, and she was strong-willed and smart, up to a point, of course, because if she'd been really smart, she wouldn't have gotten involved with me. She was fun, but responsible too, and she had an amazing gift for happiness. I don't think we were too bad for each other. We got on well, we started going out, and after a few months we got married. We had a child, and when the boy was two years old, we got divorced. She introduced me to the world of adults, although I only realized that after we split up. With Lola, I was an adult, living among adults; I had adult problems and desires, and reacted like an adult; even the reasons for our separation were unambiguously adult. The aftermath was long and sometimes painful, but the upside was that it brought a degree of uncertainty back into my life, which is what I had really been missing. Did I mention that Lola's boss was Enric Rosquelles? In the time we lived together, I got a sense of what he was like. Repulsive. A toy-size tyrant full of fears and obsessions, who thought he was the center of the world, when he was just a foul, pouting lard-ass. As it turned out, he took an instant and instinctive dislike to me. We only saw each other three times and I didn't do anything to justify his hostility, which was, I discovered, irrational and unflagging. In his underhanded way he tried to trip me up on numerous occasions: keeping a close eye on my trading hours, checking my registration with the Tax Department, sending out the labor inspectors, but it was all in vain. What lay behind such persistent persecution? I can only suppose it was some casual observation, some tactless remark I made without thinking, which must have offended him deeply. I'm guessing that Lola was present, and the rest of the Social Services team. I vaguely remember a party, what was I doing there? I don't know, I must have gone with Lola, which is odd, because we didn't socialize much as a couple: she had her friends from work, including Rosquelles; and I had Alex and the deeply sad characters who drank at the Cartago. Anyhow, I probably offended him. For someone like Rosquelles, a single slightly malicious remark, barely tinged with cruelty, can be enough to nourish a lifelong grudge. But his antagonism was confined to the purely bureaucratic domain. At least until last summer. Then, incomprehensibly, he started going crazy. His behavior went over the top, and according to Lola, the staff in his department couldn't wait to go on vacation. His prejudice against South Americans had a particular focus. Day after day, night after night, I could sense the restless presence of his shadow, the hateful fluttering of a winged pig, as if this time the trap would spring shut. It was an interesting situation, in a way, and would have rewarded closer scrutiny, but all I could think about at the time was Nuria Martí. Rosquelles was clearly disturbed and foaming at the mouth, but what was that to me? It could have been an amusing variation on the love triangle, if death hadn't butted in. The way I see it now, all those years of minding my own business in Z were just a preparation for finding the body . . .

The opera singer was never an official resident of the campground

The opera singer was never an official resident of the campground; her name did not appear on the register at reception, and she never paid a peseta to sleep there, or anywhere else for that matter. The cleaning ladies didn't know about her, nor did the receptionists; just El Carajillo and me. Her name was Carmen, and from the beginning of spring to the middle of fall, she spent her days in Z, sleeping wherever she could, wherever she was left in peace, under the ice cream stands on the beach, or in the apartment buildings' enclosures for trash cans. El Carajillo knew her well and seemed to like her, though he didn't give much away when I tried to find out more; they must have been about the same age, and sometimes that's enough to create a bond. She supported herself by singing in the cafés and streets of the historic center. Her varied repertoire was all she remembered of her glory days, so she said. Naples was the name of her absolute triumph, the culmination of a splendid and terrible period, which she never recounted in detail, beyond saying that she sang both Mozart and José Alfredo Jiménez. Her efforts were rewarded with hundred-peseta coins. The relationship between Carmen and the girl seemed to be based on a strange pact of loyalty rather than friendship. Sometimes they seemed to be mother and daughter, or grandmother and granddaughter, sometimes they were more like statues accidentally set down side by side. The girl, who went by the name of Caridad, smuggled the old lady in every night under El Carajillo's indulgent gaze. They shared a tent next to the pétanque ground, and were both in the habit of going to bed late and sleeping in. It wasn't hard to pick out their tent from a distance: all around it, like the turrets of a miserable fortress, were little foot-high pyramids of rubbish, or rather of sundry used and useless objects which they hadn't quite thrown away. To be honest, it's a miracle that we weren't continually flooded with complaints. Maybe Caridad's neighbors didn't think it was worth it, since they were just passing through, or maybe they had given up. In reception there was a list of clients who were behind in their payments; Caridad was at the top of it (with two months' due) and according to the Peruvian she would soon be asked to leave. Wouldn't it be better to offer her a job? That's what the receptionists thought, but it was Bobadilla's decision, and apparently he was scared of her. According to the Peruvian, you could often tell she was carrying a knife. I didn't want to believe him but was haunted, in spite of my skepticism, by an evocative image: Caridad wandering through the town (which I hardly knew, since I rarely left the campground), with a kitchen knife under her T-shirt, lost in blurry-eyed contemplation of something that nobody else could make out. The knife had a history, as I later discovered. Caridad had come to Stella Maris with a boyfriend, before the beginning of the season. They spent the first days looking for work. It was a month of record rains, according to El Carajillo (I was in Barcelona at the time and I vaguely remember the sound of the rain beating against the window of my room), and that was when Caridad started coughing and looking ill. She and her boyfriend had no money and basically lived on yogurt and fruit. Sometimes they got drunk on beer and spent the whole day cooped up in their tent, whining and whispering sweet nothings. Then they found work washing dishes in the kitchen of a bar on the Paseo Marítimo, but two weeks later Caridad came back to the campground in the middle of the day, and never went back to work. Soon after that the fights began. One night they chased each other down to the reeds. El Carajillo heard something and left the office and walked around the swimming pool to see what was going on. He found Caridad lying in a heap, covered in scratches and hardly breathing. She wasn't dead, as he thought at first; her eyes were open and she was looking at the grass and the sandy ground. It took her a while to realize that someone was trying to help her. Sometimes cries came from their tent, and it was hard to tell for sure if they were cries of pain or joy. The boy was pale and always wore long-sleeved shirts. He had a motorbike, on which they had arrived at the campground, but after that they hardly used it. Caridad liked walking, walking aimlessly, or remaining absolutely still; and maybe he preferred not to spend money on gas. Both of them were under twenty and they both had a look of utter hopelessness about them. One night Caridad turned up on the terrace with a knife, alone; the next morning her friend left Stella Maris and didn't come back. Or that was the most popular version of the story—the one Bobadilla heard when he came in the afternoon to cast an eye over the accounts and give them his blessing. Caridad didn't spend much time at the campground. One night El Carajillo saw her come in with Carmen but didn't say anything. The following night he said he would turn a blind eye, on one condition: that the old woman didn't sing. The relationship between the two women was compounded of chance and necessity: Carmen paid for the coffees, Caridad provided a place to sleep; during the day they kept each other company and wandered all over Z. The old woman sang her heart out, while Caridad observed the people, the umbrellas, the tables covered with drinks. Both of them hated the beach and the sun. One time the old lady, who was the only one who spoke, confessed to me that they swam at night, in the rock pools, completely naked. Moonlight is good for the skin, cutie! In the early hours of the morning, as I listened to El Carajillo snoring, I imagined Caridad kneeling naked on the sand, waiting for a cough that seemed to be rising out of the sea. I never managed to make her smile, although I tried everything I could think of. Before starting work I would buy beer, sandwiches and potato chips at the local supermarket so I could invite them to join me for a meal on the terrace at night. Once I waited for them with a tub of ice cream and three plastic spoons. The ice cream had pretty much melted but we ate it anyway. The old lady thanked me for those attentions by pinching me on the arm and calling me nicknames. Caridad seemed to be watching a film projected in the sky. As the days went by, summer brought a full contingent of tourists to Z, and I had less and less time to spend with them. As the campers arrived, the women seemed to withdraw, fading from the world. One night I found out that Bobadilla and the Peruvian had kicked them out. El Carajillo got away with a reprimand, and that was the end of it. Their tent was in the storeroom, held as security until they paid off their debt. That night I slipped into the storeroom unobserved and searched with my flashlight until I found it, bundled in a corner. I sat down beside it and put my fingers into the folds of the cloth. There was a smell of petrol. I thought I would never see them again . . .

ENRIC ROSQUELLES:

I found a plumber, an electrician, a carpenter

I found a plumber, an electrician, and a carpenter, and put them to work under the supervision of the only builder in Z I could trust, a ruthless mean individual: the Palacio Benvingut project was up and running. I bled money from stones; no one bothered to check on where the consignments or parts of consignments were going. Suspicion is a way of life in this town but nobody dared to suspect me. I didn't lie, or not systematically. I managed to convince Pilar and three councilors that my project would be good for the town. The builder didn't know the real purpose of the work (he was right-wing, very right-wing, and I was always afraid he would try to blackmail me). Why did I use him and not someone else? Anyone else would have talked, of course. I found the design I was looking for in a library in Barcelona. I copied it patiently by hand, until I understood how it all worked. Soon the workmen arrived and electricity returned to the Palacio Benvingut. Then I publicly announced the objectives and the extent of the restoration that had been undertaken, but in a vague and low-key way, after all the project was still in its early stages. I estimated that the work would take five years to complete, and foresaw that when completed the facility would be of benefit to the following departments: Social Services, Education, Fairs and Festivals, Culture, Health (!), Community Affairs, Child Welfare, and Security (!). I'm sorry,

I can't help laughing. How could they have swallowed everything I told them? It's a testament to human gullibility. The only person who said anything was some sad pencil-pusher from Fairs and Festivals who asked me (without any malicious intent, as I have since realized) if I was planning to build a nuclear shelter in the palace's rock foundations. I looked daggers at him and the poor man regretted having opened his mouth. They were all so naïve and stupid! I achieved my goal in less than a year. For the sake of appearances and because in the long term I really was planning to open the palace to the public (even if no one believes me now), I kept on a couple of unemployed men who worked from eight in the morning till two in the afternoon, cleaning up the other wings of the building. They did almost nothing, of course, and I knew it, but I let them be. From time to time, I sent out a van loaded with paint or planks, or had the old ping-pong table from the drop-in center moved to one of the salons in the palace, just to keep things moving a bit. Pilar is clever, but even she didn't suspect anything. The communists and the Convergencia i Unión councilors thought it would win us votes in the next elections. Now everyone's saying the opposite, but at the time they were swayed by my confidence; my willpower was irresistible. There seemed to be no end to the pleasure coursing through every cell of my body. Pleasure blended with fear, I admit, as if I had just been born. I had never felt better in my life, that's the truth. If ghosts exist, Benvingut's ghost was by my side . . .

REMO MORÁN:

I met Nuria through the Z Environmental Group

I met Nuria through the Z Environmental Group, whose ten members, at the most, usually met in cafés in winter and on the terraces of hotels or bars in summer. They didn't meet in August, because everyone was on vacation. Alex knew some of the members, and so did a friend of Nuria's, or something like that. One night the Del Mar was the designated meeting place, and since I live there, we were bound to see each other. Nuria was sitting by the window. Our eyes met as I came out from behind the bar with a tray of beers, and from that moment until Alex introduced me to the whole club, we couldn't stop looking at each other. I decided to stay and listen to them talking about the state of Z's beaches and gardens. Later I tagged along when they went to a disco in Y, where some lunar or solar festival was being celebrated. Neither Nuria nor I had been to one of these meetings before. As fate would have it, we came back from Y together, with Alex and another guy, and one of them suggested we stop at a cove, wade out into the water and wait for dawn. In the end only Nuria and I went swimming; Alex was too drunk and stayed in the car, while the other guy just sat on the sand with his legs crossed, meditating on dark forms or maybe feasting his eyes on Nuria's legs and the rest of her incredible body. Is it possible to swim and talk at the same time? Yes, it is, of course it is. I have to say I'm not in good physical shape; I smoke two

packs a day and don't exercise, but that morning I followed
Nuria two or three hundred yards out into the sea, maybe
even four hundred, or more, and I thought I wouldn't be
able to make it back. Her hair got wet progressively, section
by section, like the sculpted hair of a statue, and when the
sun began to rise, her head was the brightest thing on that
ominous sea that was sucking me down. When we were
splitting up, Lola had said to me: Get yourself a pretty girl,
a daddy's girl, but hurry, before you get old. It's not the
cruelest parting shot I've heard. Out there in the sea, convinced I was going to sink, I remembered Lola's words, and
they hurt, because Nuria didn't have a father, she couldn't
be a daddy's girl. We had spoken at the disco, but it was
almost impossible to hear anything; so I could say that we
had our first real conversation in the sea, and the feeling I
had then, the conviction that I wouldn't make it back to
shore, the intimation of death by drowning under a matte-
blue sky, a sky that looked like a lung in a tub of blue paint,
persisted throughout all our subsequent conversations.
I returned to the shore on my back, very slowly, feeling
Nuria's hands supporting my shoulders from time to time.
As she was helping me, she talked about the good things,
the things she believed were worth fighting and working
for. I remember she mentioned a pool and the swimming
lessons she had taken at the age of five. They had paid off:
she was a fantastic swimmer! By the time we reached the
shore, the sky had turned from blue to pink, the pink of
an enlightened butcher. That afternoon, taking a siesta as
usual in my hotel room, I dreamed of her hot-and-cold
smile and woke up shouting. Three days later, at lunchtime, she turned up at the Del Mar and sat down at my
table. She had already eaten, but accepted a coffee, without
sugar, and left half of it. I soon discovered that she was

extremely particular about what she ate. She was five foot seven inches tall, and weighed a hundred and twenty-one pounds. In the morning she got up early and went running for half an hour to an hour; she played tennis regularly, and had studied classical and modern dance. She didn't drink or smoke. She knew what proteins, minerals and vitamins each sort of food contains, as well as its calorific value. She was in her freshman year at the National Institute of Physical Education, although she added sadly that she should have been a junior, but training and competitions had got in the way. It took me quite a long time to find out what kind of training and competitions, not for lack of interest on my part, on the contrary, but because she preferred to talk about other things. We stayed at the table until the only people left in the dining room were some old ladies dressed in white, who soon moved out onto the terrace to crochet. When I had finished my vanilla ice cream (Nuria rejected all the desserts on the menu with a smile), we went up to my room and made love. We said goodbye at six in the evening. I went down with her to the street, where she had left her shiny, chrome-plated racing bike. Before getting on, she tied back her hair with a black ribbon and said she'd call me. All I could find to say was that she could call whenever she liked, any time, day or night. I probably sounded too eager. It made her uncomfortable and she looked away. I had the impression she thought I was going too fast. Are you in love with me? Don't fall in love, don't fall in love, she seemed to be trying to say to me. I felt vulnerable and embarrassed like an adolescent . . .

GASPAR HEREDIA:

I got into the habit of walking around town

I got into the habit of walking around town in the vague hope of running into Caridad. By then Z was already full of tourists and the streets were buzzing all the time. El Carajillo soon realized that after we had breakfast in a cantina near the campground, I was heading into town, instead of going back to my tent to sleep. But I couldn't find a trace of Caridad, and even the old opera singer, who by all accounts earned her living in the street, seemed to have disappeared. A few times I thought I heard her voice coming from a terrace or an alley and ran to find her, but it would be some traveler singing to pay her way, or Rocío Jurado on the radio. My routine began to change. I worked from ten at night till eight in the morning and slept from midday to six in the evening, although with the massive influx of tourists it wasn't easy to sleep. I went to bed later and later until my bedtime coincided with the beginning of my shift. El Carajillo noticed the change, of course, and didn't mind if I neglected my watchman's duties in order to catch up on sleep: I slept in one of the leather armchairs in the office for one or two hours at a time, and between naps I did rounds of the campground, inevitably ending up at the place where Caridad's tent had been pitched. I would sit down there under a pine tree, beside the pétanque ground, with my flashlight switched off, and I could see her blurry eyes and her angular silhouette disappearing towards the fence and the headlights of the cars driving past outside. When you're down like that, reading poetry's no help. Nor is getting drunk. Or crying. Or finding something else to worry about. So I resumed my walks around Z with fresh vigor, and rearranged my routine: I slept from nine in the morning till three in the afternoon, and as soon as I woke up (hot, sweating and feeling like I'd been buried) I would slip out, bypassing reception so they wouldn't see me and give me some chore (there were always plenty waiting to be done). Once outside I felt free, and walked quickly down the avenue past the other campgrounds to the Paseo Marítimo, and then into the historic center, where I had my breakfast in peace while reading the paper. Right after that I would start looking for them, supposing that Caridad and Carmen were still together, combing the neighborhoods of Z from north to south, from east to west, always in vain, mumbling to myself and remembering things it would have been better to forget, making plans, imagining I was back in Mexico, enveloped in an unmistakably Mexican energy, eventually concluding that both of them had left town. But one day, on the way back to the campground I stopped on the esplanade beside the port, and saw her: she was in the crowd that had gathered near the beach to watch a hang-gliding competition. I recognized her immediately. I felt good in the pit of my stomach; I wanted to go over and touch her back with my finger. But something warned me not to, something I couldn't pin down at the time. A semicircle of spectators, all staring up into the sky, had gathered around the jury's dais; I stayed on the edge of the crowd. A red hang glider, the color of its sail matching the sunset sky, took off from the hill overlooking the town; it glided down over the slopes of the hill, then rose before reaching the fishing port, flew over the yacht club, and seemed for a moment to be heading east over the sea. The pilot, a dark, hunched figure, was barely visible because of the angle of the glider. At the castle up on the hill, another competitor was already preparing for take-off. I had never seen anything like it. Suddenly I felt absolutely at ease among the growing shadows, which were gradually joining up to construct a real darkness within the summer night. I could have passed for a tourist; in any case, no one was paying me any attention. By this stage the red hang glider was only a few yards from the circular target on the beach; there were a few shouts of encouragement as he came in to land. Then the white hang glider pushed off from the castle; the last competitor was a Frenchman, so the loudspeaker informed us. Suddenly a breeze lifted him high above the launch ramp. Caridad was wearing a black, long-sleeved shirt and black pants; like everyone else she had turned her gaze from the pilot who was landing to the one who had just taken off, who seemed to be having some trouble controlling his glider. Something about Caridad, something about her back and her hair, triggered a familiar but brief and almost imperceptible feeling of strangeness and danger. I could tell from the applause that the pilot of the red hang glider had landed. I decided to go a little closer. The three judges on the dais were looking at their watches and cracking jokes; they were all very young. Along the esplanade, groups of boys and girls were ceremoniously packing away the previous competitors' equipment. A guy who I guessed was a pilot, though certainly not the one who had just landed, was sitting on the sand, very near the water's edge, with his hands on his knees, hanging his head. Next to me someone remarked that the white hang glider was coming in to land from the hill instead of from the sea. I thought I could see signs of anxiety, and of pleasure, on the faces of the better informed spectators. That was clearly not the right way to approach the strip of beach where the judges were waiting. Up in the air, the pilot tried to steer his craft toward the port so he could go out over the sea, but he was losing altitude and couldn't seem to correct his trajectory. I moved away from the crowd and tried to find a place in the garden by the esplanade from which I could go on watching Caridad. Children were playing among the hedges and flowerpots, oblivious to what was happening on the beach; trios of old timers were sitting on the benches, looking at the masts of the yachts, which rose over the top of the long wall hiding the pier. Suddenly the white hang glider began to rise again, and for a moment it hung directly above the swelling crowd, so people had to tip their heads right back to see it. That white, inert object seemed to be climbing higher and higher, as if it was enclosed in a tube of air. That was when Caridad left the group of spectators. A man beside me, leading a little girl and boy by the hand, pointed out that the pilot was kicking his legs; he was obviously beyond caring about sporting decorum. I crossed the garden, heading for the restaurants, against the tide of people coming the other way, who had settled up hurriedly or even left their tables without paying; most of them were still holding their glasses as they rushed to see the pilot hanging in the air, although from where I was he could barely be glimpsed through the branches of the trees. Then I saw her again: she was standing with her back to the sea, looking at the front of a restaurant, very quietly, as if she had no intention of crossing the street. Was she waiting for someone? And what was that under her shirt, sticking up from her belt? When Caridad rushed toward the Paseo and disappeared into a side street, I knew without a doubt (or rather with a shudder and a clenching in my gut) that what she had under her shirt was a knife. I set off after her just as the pilot came spinning down out of control, falling toward the beach and the screaming spectators. I didn't look back. I crossed the Paseo and went down a narrow street lined with apartment buildings. A group of middle-aged French tourists, all dressed up for a party, came out of a gateway and for a moment I thought I had lost her. But when I got to the corner, there she was, standing in front of a video-game arcade. All I could do was stop and wait. An ambulance with its siren wailing went past a few yards away, for the pilot, no doubt. Was he dead? Or seriously injured? Without warning, or any sign that she had seen me, Caridad set off again, but kept stopping in front of every shop, even at the doors of restaurants, of which there were fewer as we went away from the beach. I have to admit it occurred to me that I might be following a mugger. Withdrawal symptoms, desperate theft. If an assault was committed, I'd be in a delicate position. They'd have to suspect me of complicity. I thought about my papers—my nonexistent papers—and wondered what I could invent for the police. Twenty yards away, Caridad stopped a passerby, asked him the time (he looked at her as if she was from another planet), then turned left, heading for the fishermen's wharf. But well before that, when she got to the Paseo de la Maestranza, she stopped and sat down on the seawall. That posture, with her legs hanging down and her back hunched, made the shape of the knife more obvious. But with night coming on, the color of her shirt would help to keep it hidden. I snuck in between some boats that were being repaired and lit a cigarette; I had no idea what time it was, but I felt relaxed. From my hideout I could watch her at my leisure, without risk: she seemed terribly sad, like a tree that had suddenly sprouted from the seawall, a mystery of nature. And yet, when some precise spring-loaded mechanism set her in motion again, that impression disappeared, leaving only a trace like a blurred photo and one thing for sure: solitude. Caridad went back the way she had come, but on the opposite side-walk this time, weaving through the café tables, sometimes going into the places that were busy and too brightly lit, with a leisurely elastic rhythm that revealed strength and a dancer's resolve at odds with the extreme slenderness of her limbs. I almost lost her on one of those terraces; she went in while I stayed outside, hidden by the menu board, and suddenly I saw Remo Morán, who was sitting at one of the tables with two very suntanned guys. I felt trapped; I should have been at work by then, and Remo's gaze reared up like ectoplasm and hit me between the eyes, or that's how it felt, but in fact it was a sleeper's or a dreamer's gaze—he didn't seem to be listening to the suntanned guys, and at the time I thought, Either he's critically ill or he's very happy. Any-way, I turned around, crossed the Paseo and waited in the gardens. Soon it began to drizzle. When Caridad came out of the restaurant, there was something different about her step; it was longer and more decisive, as if the stroll was over and now she was in a hurry. I followed her without hesitation (but hadn't anyone in the restaurant noticed that she was carrying a knife?) and we began to leave the bright lights of the center behind us. We went through the fisher-men's neighborhood, climbed a steep street lined with ter-raced houses, at the end of which was a dirty, modern, four-storey school, with that unfinished look that schools always have, and then, beyond the last buildings, we set out on the highway that runs around the coves, heading for Y. From time to time headlights lit up Caridad's shrunken sil-houette, pressing on relentlessly. Twice I heard men's voices yelling from cars, but they didn't stop. Maybe they saw me. Maybe they saw Caridad and were scared. Only the wind in the trees stayed with us until the end. We walked a long way. At each bend in the road, the sea appeared, streaked with a milky brightness, the sea with its clouds and its rocks, lapping the sandy beaches of Z. When she reached the third cove, Caridad left the highway and turned off onto a dirt road. It had stopped raining and the mansion was visible from a distance. I tripped over something and fell down. Caridad stopped for a few moments at the iron gate, before opening it and disappearing. I picked myself up carefully; my legs were shaking. There were no lights shining in the house to suggest that it was occupied. The iron gate had remained ajar. Peering in, I could barely make out the remains of an enormous garden, a half-ruined fountain and weeds growing everywhere. A paved path led to a kind of dilapidated porch on various levels. There I discovered that the front door was also open, and I thought I heard a sound, a very faint sound of music that could only have been coming from inside the mansion. That was what I concluded as I stood there on the porch like a rain-wet statue, with my left hand resting on the door frame and my right hand cupped to my ear, before finally deciding to go in. The hall, or what I presumed was a hall, empty except for some boxes piled up in a corner, led to a glass door. When my eyes had adjusted to the darkness, I proceeded with caution, trying to make as little noise as possible. When I opened the glass door, I could hear the music clearly. A few paces further on, the corridor branched. I chose to go left. On one side of the passage there were doors, but although they were open, the rooms were utterly black. There was some light in the passage itself, coming in through a long window on the other side, running right along the wall and looking into an interior courtyard, which seemed to be at a much lower level than the front garden. The passage finally opened out into a circular room like the cockpit of an impossible submarine, from which one stairway led up to the floor above and another led down to the sunken garden. That was where the music was coming from. So down I went. The floor was marble and the walls were decorated with plaster reliefs, which neglect had rendered indecipherable. Something moved in the weeds. A rat, maybe. But my attention was now focused on a double door. The music was coming through it along with a freezing draft that dried the sweat on my face in an instant. Behind that door, illuminated by four spotlights hanging from huge beams, a girl was skating on an ice rink . . .

ENRIC ROSQUELLES:

I would leave the car parked under the old vine arbor

I would leave the car parked under the old vine arbor, Benvingut's Roman arbor, which had resisted the passage of time and was still there, covered in dust but standing firm. Nuria would arrive around seven, on her bike, and I was almost always by the door, sitting on a wicker chair that I had found in one of the rooms and cleaned and disinfected, before placing it in a cool shady place from which I could spy Nuria's bicycle when it first appeared on the highway to Y; then it would be hidden for a while by trees, before reappearing on the long road that led straight up to the palace. Once the rink was finished we saw each other every day of course. I would usually bring some fruit—apricots, grapes, pears—a thermos of strong tea, and the radio cassette player that Nuria used for training. She brought a sports bag with her costume and skates, and a bottle of water. She also used to bring books of poetry, a new one every three days or so, which she would browse through during her breaks, leaning against one of the many cases I had decided to leave inside the big shed, so as not to arouse suspicion. Who else knew about the existence of the rink? Well, no one and everyone, in a sense. Everyone in Z knew something or other, but no one was smart enough to put the pieces of information together and form a coherent whole. It was easy to fool them. Actually, I don't think anyone really cared what was happening with the mansion or the money. Or, no, they did care about the money, of course they did, but not enough to work overtime trying to find out where it had gone. In any case, I was always careful. Not even Nuria knew everything; I told her the rink would be a public facility, and that put an end to her questions, although it was obvious that we were the only ones using the Palacio Benvingut for the duration of that summer. Nuria had her own problems, of course, and I respected that. They say love makes people generous. I'm not so sure; it made me generous with Nuria, but no one else. With other people I became wary and selfish, petty and malicious, perhaps because I knew what a treasure I possessed (a treasure of immaculate purity) and couldn't help comparing my situation to the filth in which they were all wallowing. I can confidently say that there has been nothing in my life to match the suppers or dinners we had together on the steps leading down from the palace to the sea. Nuria had a way of eating fruit while gazing at the horizon that was, I don't know, unique. And the view was truly exceptional. We hardly spoke. I would sit on the next step down and look at her now and again (looking for too long could be painful), sipping and savoring my tea. Nuria had two track suits, a blue one with diagonal white stripes, which was, I think, the official tracksuit of the Olympic skating team, and a jet black one, a gift from her mother, which set off her blonde hair and her perfect complexion: she looked like a Botticelli angel flushed with exertion. Instead of looking at her, I looked at the tracksuits, and I still remember every fold, every wrinkle, the way the blue one bulged at the knees, the delicious scent that the black one gave off when Nuria was wearing it and the evening breeze made words superfluous. A scent of vanilla, a scent of lavender. Next to her, I must have looked out of place. You have to remember I came straight from work to our daily meetings, and sometimes I didn't have time to change out of my suit and tie. But when Nuria was late, I'd get some jeans from the trunk of the car and a thick, loose-fitting Snyder sweatshirt, and take off my shoes and put on some Di Albi mocassins, which are supposed to be worn without socks, although I sometimes forgot. I did all this under the arbor, sweating and listening to the insects. I never put on my tracksuit when she was around. Tracksuits make me look twice as fat as I am, they expand my waist mercilessly, and I fear they even make me look shorter. Once Nuria tried to get me to skate with her for a while. Excuse me for laughing. I guess she wanted to see me in the middle of the rink, which is why she brought another pair of skates that evening and absolutely insisted that I put them on. She even lied, Nuria, who never told a lie, she said that for the routine she wanted to practice, she needed somebody beside her. I had never seen her behave like that, like a spoilt, sulky child, like a tyrannical princess, but I put it down to tired-ness, boredom and maybe nervous tension. Her big day was approaching, and although I told her that she was skating wonderfully, who was I, really, to judge? In any case, I never put on the skates. Out of cowardice, fear of ridicule or fall-ing over, or because the rink was there for her benefit, not mine. But I did occasionally dream I was skating. If you've got time I can tell you about it. Not that there's much to tell: I was simply there, in the middle of the rink, with skates on my feet, and all the building work I had been planning on before they found me out was complete: comfortable new seats on both sides of the rink, showers, massage tables, an immaculate dressing room, and I could skate, I could spin and leap, I was moving smoothly over the ice, riding on ab-solute silence . . .

REMO MORÁN:

I have very few clear memories of Nuria's second visit to the hotel

I have very few clear memories of Nuria's second visit to the hotel. She came to the Del Mar at lunchtime, like before, but didn't have coffee or want to go up to my room. She felt claustrophobic in the hotel, so we went for a drive. When we got into the car, I was the one feeling claustrophobic; I'm a terrible driver, I don't like cars, and although I own one, it's mainly used for transporting supplies to the hotel, and I don't even do that myself. For a while we drove around aimlessly on inland roads; the heat was stifling and we sweated profusely, not saying a word. With a sudden sinking feeling I thought she might have come to split up with me. Pines, orchards, empty riding schools and old wholesale pottery stores slid by so slowly it was excruciating. Finally, between yawns, Nuria suggested we go back to the hotel. When we got there, we went straight up to my room. I remember her skin under the hot shower. I was outside, but because of the steam I was dripping with sweat. She had her eyes shut tightly, as if there was something only she could sense in between the drops of water. As if the numberless scalding droplets were launching an attack on her skin. The water dripping from her perfect legs left a wet trail across the tiles. I put on the air conditioning and watched her go out onto the balcony and look at the sea. Before getting into bed, she cast an eye over my bookshelves and the wardrobes. There wasn't much to see. I'm looking for microphones, she explained. Nuria's movements had the peculiar property of continuing to vibrate faintly in a room, or so it seemed, long after she had gone. She cried underneath me, unexpectedly, and that made me stop straight away. Am I hurting you? Go on, she said. Once I would have collected her tears with the tip of my tongue, but the years leave their mark, they paralyze you. It was as if a kick in the ass had sent me flying into another room where there was no need for air conditioning. I opened the curtains, just a little, called the restaurant and asked them to bring up two cups of tea with lemon; then I sat down on the edge of the bed and stroked her shoulder, not knowing what to do. Nuria drank the contents of the teapot, steadily, dry-eyed. At night, when I went to bed, I got into the habit of speaking as if she was there in the room with me. I called her Olympic Gold and dumb things like that, but they made me laugh and even double up with laughter sometimes, which left me feeling inwardly calm, or lucid at least, something I hadn't felt for a long time. We never talked about love, or even implied that what we did from four to seven had anything to do with love. She had gone out with a boy from Barcelona and often mentioned him. She spoke of him in a curious, distant way, as if his ghost was wandering about in the vicinity. She extolled his athletic virtues, the hours he spent at the gym, his absolute dedication. I often thought she still loved him. Some afternoons the hotel room was like a crater about to erupt. According to Alex it's impossible to maintain a relationship in the space of a room; sooner or later, one or the other is going to get bored. I agreed, but what could I do? Whenever I suggested going out, she said no; in the evening she was too tired, or something, and I didn't really feel like doing the rounds of the discos either. One night, though, about two weeks after we met, we did go out, and it was great. A brief but joyful excursion. When I was taking her back to her place (she never invited me in), I said that I found her beauty unnerving. A rash confession, because I knew it was something she didn't like to talk about. In retrospect her reply stands out as the most significant moment of that night. (We spent the rest of it laughing continuously.) In a vehement tone of voice that banished all doubt, she said that the most beautiful woman she had ever met was an East German skater, the world champion, Marianne something. That was all, but it took me aback. Nuria was obviously a girl who knew exactly what she wanted. Another afternoon she asked me, with what I took to be genuine curiosity, what I was doing in Z, a backwater without a bookshop or a decent cinema. I said it was because of my businesses (an abject lie). Your business is literature, and that's why you should be living in Barcelona or Madrid. But then I wouldn't see you any more, I replied. That was going to happen anyway, she told me, because hopefully she'd soon be back on the Olympic skating team and have her grant again. And what will you do if that doesn't work out? Nuria looked at me as if I was a child, and shrugged her shoulders. Finish my course at the Institute, maybe, give skating classes in some big city in Europe or at a North American university; but deep down she was sure she would get back on the team. That's what I'm working toward, she said, that's why I'm training hard . . .

Gaspar Heredia:

The music was the "Fire Dance"

The music was the "Fire Dance," by Manuel de Falla, and I could see the skater's torso moving in time with it as she lifted her arms, doing a clumsy yet somehow affecting imitation of a devotee offering a gift to a tiny invisible deity. The rest—the ice, the girl's legs, her silver skates—were mainly hidden by piles of packing cases left there to block the way and make the place look like an amphitheater when viewed from the rink, although as I made my way around them, they seemed to form something more like a miniature labyrinth. For a start all I could see was the girl's back, her arms curved in an ethereal embrace and the spotlights shining onto the ice, which reminded me of the lights around a boxing ring in Tijuana. The floor was made of cement, sloping down slightly towards the center, and the walls had been built on a foundation of irregularly shaped rocks, black with smoke. I threaded my way among the packing cases, some of which still had the dispatch documents on them, until I could find a better observation post. At the edge of the illuminated area, a fat guy was sitting on a multicolored beach chair, busily reading documents and annotating them with a felt-tip pen; at his feet was a cassette player, with the volume turned up, broadcasting the notes of the "Fire Dance" to every corner of the shed. The fat guy seemed very absorbed in what he was doing, although from time to time he looked up at the skater. The spotlights revealed something that intensified my bewilderment: in one corner of the rink was a ladder going down through the ice, and tangled around the ladder was a bunch of colored cables, which also went down through the bluish-white layer on which the curious skater was executing her figures. In spite of the cold I felt drops of sweat running down my face. Suddenly, the fat guy said something. The girl went on skating, oblivious. The fat guy spoke again, at greater length this time, and the girl, who was skating backwards now, replied with a curt sentence, as if what he had said didn't concern her. Partly because they were speaking Catalan and partly because I was very nervous, I couldn't understand what they were saying, but I felt as if I was inside a cave. The skater started practicing little jumps and kneeling moves; then the fat guy's shadow emerged from the darkness and approached the edge of the rink. There he stood still with his hands in his pockets, his remarkably round head turning slowly, as he followed the girl with his shining, intent, unblinking eyes. There was something disturbing about that odd couple—the girl all grace and speed, the bottom-heavy man like a lead-weighted doll—but watching them I also felt a kind of silent fierce joy, which helped me not to lose my nerve and run away. I knew that they couldn't see me, and that Caridad was somewhere around, so I settled down to wait as long as it would take. The skater began to turn on the spot, in the middle of rink, spinning faster and faster. With her chin up, her legs together and her back curved, she looked at first like an elegant spinning top. All at once, just as the fat guy and I were both, I presume, expecting the routine to end, she shot away toward the edge of the rink, in a move that although perfectly controlled seemed to owe more to luck than to training. The fat guy clapped. Marvelous, marvelous, he said in Catalan. I can understand words like that (*meravellós*). The skater went round the rink twice more before stopping in front of the fat guy, who was waiting with a towel. Then I heard the cassette player clicking off and the fat guy went back into the semidarkness and turned around while the skater got changed. In fact all she did was put on a tracksuit over her leotard, but nevertheless, he kept his gaze chastely averted. After putting her skates in a sports bag, the skater said something I didn't catch. Her voice was like velvet. The fat guy turned around and, as if measuring his steps, approached the brightly lit sector. How was it? she asked, looking down, in a different tone of voice. Marvelous. You don't think it was too slow? No, not for me, but if you think so . . . They were both smiling, but in very different ways. The girl sighed. I'm exhausted, she said. Will you take me home? Of course, stuttered the fat guy, his lips curved in a shy smile. Wait for me in the passage, I'll go and turn off the lights. The girl left without saying a word. The fat guy went behind a pile of cases and moments later the whole rink was plunged in complete darkness. He appeared again finding his way with a flashlight, and went out. I heard them go up the stairs. What do I do now, I wondered. There were some dim points of light above me. The moon shining through holes in the roof? Disoriented fireflies more likely. It was only then that I noticed the sound of a generator operating at full capacity somewhere in the mansion. To keep the ice frozen? Still confused about what I was doing there, I sat down on the freezing ground, leaned against a case and tried to think straight. But I couldn't. A different noise, not the generator, put me on my guard. Someone lit a match at the edge of the rink and shadows immediately began to dance on the walls of the storehouse. I got up and looked at the rink, which was like a mirror now: Caridad was standing there with the lit match in one hand and the knife in the other. Luckily the match soon went out and the return of darkness reassured me. She had probably hidden in one of the rooms until then and come to check that the skater and the fat guy were gone. She was a trespasser in that warren of a house, like me. When she lit the second match I realized she was on the lookout, and I felt bad about staying in my hiding place, but I was worried that my sudden appearance might frighten her and make things worse. My decision not to reveal myself was also influenced the color of the knife-blade, which matched the color of the ice. After faltering repeatedly, the second match went out, but this time there was no interval of darkness; she lit another straight away and, as if succumbing to an attack of vertigo, stepped back suddenly, away from the edge of the rink. The third match soon went out, and its death was accompanied by a sigh. Only once had I ever heard anyone sigh like that: a hard, harsh sigh, alive in every hair, and the mere memory of it made me feel ill. I squatted between the cases until all I could hear was the generator and my own uneven breathing. I chose not to move for a long time. When I noticed that one of my legs was becoming seriously numb, I began the retreat; it was all I could do not to panic and go running down the mansion's twisting corridors. Surprisingly I found my way without the slightest difficulty. The front door was locked. I jumped out a window. Once in the garden, I didn't even try to open the iron gate; without a second thought I scaled the wall as if my life depended on it . . .

We started training at the beginning of summer

We started training at the beginning of summer. Sorry, Nuria started training at the beginning of summer, and we both thought that if she worked hard in July, August and September, she would triumph at the national trials, to be held some time in October in Madrid. No matter how corrupt the trainers, judges and administrators, Nuria's virtuosity or finesse or whatever you like to call it, consolidated or perfected during those months of training, was bound to leave them speechless, and they'd have no choice but to let her back on the Olympic team, which was going to Budapest in November, if I'm not mistaken, for the annual European Figure Skating Competition. To be frank, the prospect of not seeing Nuria for at least two months (October would be spent training intensively in Madrid, then November in Budapest) was heartbreaking. Of course I was careful not to let it show. There was also the possibility that in October she would be dropped from the team for good, but I preferred not to think about that, because I knew what a blow it would be to her, and I had no idea how she would react. I didn't want them to drop her, I swear! All I wanted was for her to be happy! That was the reason the rink had been built, so she would be able to train properly and get back on the team. With hindsight, I realize I should have hired a trainer, at least, but even if I had thought of it at the time, how could I have justified employing someone with qualifications like that? And where would I have found such a person? In summer, there's a surplus of English teachers, but not of figure-skating trainers. On one occasion, if I remember rightly, Nuria mentioned an exiled Pole, a young guy, whose contract with the Catalan Federation had been canceled after six months because of a breach of professional ethics. What had he done? Nuria didn't know, nor did she care. I confess that I imagined him having sex with, or perhaps raping, a skater, female or male, in a dressing room. Assuming the worst, as usual. In any case, the Pole was hanging around in Barcelona, and we could have sought him out, but neither of us had time, or felt like it, so we soon gave up on the idea. I don't know why, but lying awake recently, I've started thinking about that Pole. Although we never met, and never will, I feel very close to him, almost as if he were a friend. Perhaps because in a way I took on the trainer's role, and although I could never remember the names of the different moves and routines, overall, I don't think I was too bad. As a trainer, I mean, or the next best thing, a father figure most of the time. I knew how to listen, how to encourage her to persist when she was succumbing to laziness or fatigue; I knew how to inject a certain dose of method and discipline into our daily sessions. I took care of all the bothersome, peripheral tasks, so she could concentrate one hundred percent on skating. And it was my commitment to perfection (whatever the field or the task, I have always been a perfectionist) that led me to make a discovery, or a series of small discoveries, which taken together turned out to be extremely disturbing. At the start, I tried to tell myself they were illusions produced by nervous tension, although deep down I knew that I had never been less tense. Let me explain how it happened. Sometimes I got to the palace quite a long time before Nuria, and after putting on a canvas apron that I kept for odd jobs, I would set about checking the refrigeration equipment and the state of the ice. Sometimes I did a bit of sweeping, too. In one room I kept bleach, hydrochloric acid, a pair of brooms, trash bags, gloves, rags, as well as various tools. Occasionally I put a bottle with freshly picked wildflowers in the place where Nuria changed. I cleaned the heads of the cassette player with alcohol every day and made sure to rewind the cassette to the beginning of the "Fire Dance." Sometimes, if I had time to spare, I went out to the back of the house and swept the steps that led to the cove, in case Nuria wanted to go down to the beach, before or after training. There was, in short, always something to be done, and if, as a rule, I left most of the palace's rooms alone, my tidying took me to a fair part of the first and second floors, as well as the storehouse, the arbor, the sunken garden, and the gardens facing the sea. I knew those places like the back of my hand. So I was surprised to find little things, almost always pieces of trash, in places I was sure I had cleaned the previous day. Naturally my first reaction was to suspect the pair of good-for-nothings who worked for me there in the mornings, and one day I decided to take them to task. I wasn't too hard on them—I was in a hurry—but hard enough to make them think twice next time. What sort of things did I find? Scraps that ranged from hamburger remains to empty Fortuna packs (but one of the guys smoked Ducados and the other one had kicked the habit). That was all. Insignificant things, but they shouldn't have been there. One afternoon I found a bloody tissue. I picked it up, disgusted, as if it were a moribund rat, still twitching and sniffing, and threw it in the trash. Gradually I reached the conclusion that there was somebody else in the Palacio Benvingut. For three days I was on the verge of insanity. I kept thinking about Kubrick's *The Shining*; I had seen it on video at Nuria's place not long before, and my nerves were still on edge. I tried to be objective and look for logical explanations, but then, having failed to find any, I decided to face up to the problem and search the palace from top to bottom. I devoted a whole morning to the task. I found nothing, not a shred of evidence to suggest that intruders had been present. Gradually I calmed down again, reassured by the absence of fresh trash over the following days. Naturally I said nothing to Nuria and I ended up convincing myself that it had all been a figment of my fevered imagination . . .

Remo Morán:

One day Rosquelles noticed Nuria's bike in the street

One day Rosquelles noticed Nuria's bike in the street, in front of the Del Mar, and decided to go in and see what was up. To his surprise he found Nuria sitting at the bar with me, drinking mineral water. Until that day I hadn't suspected that there might be anything between them. The situation was awkward, to say the least: Rosquelles greeted me with a mixture of hatred and wariness; Nuria greeted Rosquelles with a show of impatience and, I suspect, a touch of pleasure; caught off guard, I was slow to realize that Mister Lard-Ass wasn't after me but had come to rescue his blonde angel. Unsettled by his presence, I didn't know what to say or do, at least for the first few seconds, and in that time Rosquelles took control of the situation: with a porcine smile he asked after my son's health, as if to suggest that he might be ill while I was having fun, and then he asked after the boy's poor mother, a "tireless martyr" to the cause of welfare for the underprivileged. Nuria and I had never talked about Lola, and Fatso's words pricked her curiosity. But Rosquelles went prattling on, interspersing his questions with chuckles and asides to Nuria such as, What are you doing here, What a surprise running into you, I thought someone had stolen your bike, etc, etc, all delivered in such an artificial tone of voice you could only feel sorry for the guy in the end. And of course it didn't take him long to notice that Nuria's hair was wet, and freshly washed, like mine, and I think he put two and two together. When I tried to weigh in on the conversation, Rosquelles, who had been so bubbly just a few moments before, had already slumped into a kind of torpor: he was gripping the bar with both hands, his eyes fixed on the floor, pale and shaken, as if he'd been kicked by a donkey. It was a perfect opportunity to crush him, but I chose to observe. Nuria turned away from me, and began to talk to him in a whisper, so I couldn't hear what they were saying. He nodded a number of times, with difficulty, as if he was being garroted; he seemed to be on the brink of tears when they left. I offered to help them put the bike on the roof rack, but they assured me they could manage. The next day Nuria didn't come to the hotel. I rang her apartment (for the first time) and was told that she wasn't home. I left a message for her to call me, and waited. I heard nothing for more than a week. During that time I tried to think about other things, like maybe sleeping with another girl, but all I could do was lapse into a state of depression and lethargy. In the afternoons I spoke with Lola on the telephone, although her place was only fifteen minutes from the hotel; that's how I found out that she was planning to go to Greece for a vacation, and that when she came back she would probably resign from her job with the Z City Council and take up a new position in Gerona. Lola was going out with a Basque who had recently come to the Costa Brava, a nice guy who worked in Public Administration, and it was serious. They would be going to Greece together, by car, and taking the boy. I asked her if she was happy and she said yes. I've never been so happy, she said. At night, before going up to my room, I'd have a drink with Alex and we'd talk about anything except work. I'd let Alex choose one of his favorite topics: astrology, the lemon cure, alchemy, travel in Nepal, the tarot, palm-reading. Sometimes when he was busy with the accounts (We're number thirty on the Z rich list, he'd call out from his little office next to reception, and then I'd hear him laughing to himself, a laugh of pure joy), I'd wander over to the Cartago and ask about Gasparín. The waiters told me he rarely came there, and I could never bring myself to walk on to the campground. No way, mister. That was his favorite phrase. During those days, the temperature rose to 95 degrees: a prelude to what was to follow. I must have lost two or three pounds. At night I would wake up with a suffocating feeling and go out onto the balcony. From up there, as high as I could go, the landscape took on a different appearance: the lights of Z, the zig-zag coastline, further off, the lights of Y, and then darkness, a space of darkness edged by the glow of forest fires, beyond which lay X and, further still, Barcelona. The air was so dense that when I raised my arm I felt as if I was plunging it into a living, semi-solid mass, as if it was bound in hundreds of damp leather bracelets charged with electricity. Raising both arms, like a signaler on an aircraft carrier, felt like anally and vaginally penetrating some atmospheric hallucination or extraterrestrial creature. Despite these phenomena, summer continued to bring forth tourists in abundance; for several days the streets of Z were jam-packed, and the stink of suntan lotions and coconut oil permeated every recess of the town. Finally Nuria came back to the Del Mar, at the usual time, as if nothing had happened, although I noticed that there was now something hesitant in her manner. All she said about the incident with Rosquelles was that he didn't know anything about our relationship and that it was better to keep it that way. Personally I felt I had no right, and in fact no reason, to ask any more questions. It took me a while to realize that Nuria was afraid . . .

Gaspar Heredia:

The bosses were unlikely to show up at the campground

The bosses were unlikely to show up at the campground after midnight, and anyway El Carajillo was there to cover my back. He didn't mind my starting late, especially if there was a good reason for the delay. Of course I told him that I'd finally found Caridad. When I described the mansion on the outskirts of Z, El Carajillo told me it was the Palacio Benvingut and said it would take guts to sleep in that creepy pile. He reckoned the opera singer must have been keeping Caridad company so they could protect each other. One of them, at least, was tough, he was sure of that. What did he mean? I don't know. The palace reminded El Carajillo of Remo Morán. He claimed hoarsely that Morán was like Benvingut, or would be; one day he'd go back to America with his son and that faggot Alex (Where the fuck's he from, anyway? he asked—Chile, I replied sleepily) and build a palace to dazzle the local criminals, idiots and taxpayers. Just like Benvingut did here. With black stone, if he can get it. I wish I'd had him with me in the war, he concluded with his eyes shut, although it wasn't clear whether the remark was meant to be sarcastic, insulting or complimentary, or all three. I was careful not to mention the fat guy, the skater and the ice rink that time. Was it because I distrusted El Carajillo? No, I was afraid he wouldn't believe me. Or at least that was how I explained it to myself. I stayed awake all that night, in spite of El Carajillo's peaceful snores inviting me to fall asleep. Leaning my head against the window, I watched mosquitoes orbiting the lamp at the entrance until the sun came up. I skipped breakfast, climbed into my tent at eight and slept through till five: a long sleep stained with fugitive nightmares. When I woke up, the tent smelt of sour milk and sweat. Someone was calling me; I heard my name repeated, clearly now. I crawled out with my hair stuck to my scalp and my eyes gummed up. The Peruvian, sitting on a stone outside, laughed when he saw me. Come with me to the storeroom, he said, we've got a problem. I followed him without asking any questions. We have to find the tent that belonged to the drug addict who used to shit all over the bathroom, he explained once we got into the storeroom, where both of us were bathed in a dim light, yellowed by cobwebs and all the old mattresses. Whose tent? I asked, not realizing what was going on. Why don't I go freshen up and then you can explain it to me? The Peruvian said no, we had to find the fucking tent, and then, straight away, with an energy that struck me as excessive, started rummaging through the hundreds of disused objects piled up everywhere and hanging from the wooden ceiling criss-crossed with wires: barbecue grills, gas lamps, tarpaulins, frying pans, army blankets and, against the walls, a panoply of ditch-digging tools and cardboard boxes, some still fresh and clean, others gone soft and moldy, full of useless fuses kept there for some arcane reason known only to Bobadilla. I went out without saying a word, washed my face, chest and arms, put my head under the faucet until all my hair was wet, and then, without drying myself, because I didn't have a towel handy, returned to the storeroom. You should know where it is, said the Peruvian, kneeling in front of a pile of green and white traffic signs of various kinds, arranged vertically under what seemed to be a deflated raft. I asked what the hell we were looking for and that was how I learned that Caridad's friend had come back to the campground. The debts are paid off now, said the Peruvian, and the guy wants his tent. For a moment I thought that Caridad had come with him, but the Peruvian went on to explain that the guy was on his own and hadn't even asked about his girlfriend's whereabouts. He had come to spend a few days at the campground and had paid off the debt, including the days that Caridad had been there without him. In the place where I had left the tent, I found a box of those flags that are strung up at the entrances to campgrounds in a show of internationalism; successive seasons of exposure to the weather had practically destroyed them. The Peruvian began to pull out the flags and name them one by one, nostalgically, like an ex-jailbird reciting the names of the prisons in which his youth had been consumed: Germany, Great Britain, the United States, Italy, Holland, Belgium, Switzerland, Sweden, Denmark, Canada . . . Except for the United States, I've lived in all these countries, he said. A few yards away, against a rickety wardrobe, was the tent. I cleaned it a bit with one of the flags that the Peruvian had been flapping like a bullfighter's cape, and suggested we rest for a while. The Peruvian looked at me curiously; we were both sweating and the fine dust floating in the air of the storehouse stuck to our skin, forming little lumps. We remained silent for a good while, enveloped in that yellow light, whose color, I realized then, was mainly due to the old newspapers standing in for windowpanes. Between us, like a plank buoying up two castaways, was the tent in which Caridad had slept and dreamed and made love. I would have hugged it if the Peruvian hadn't been standing there impatiently. We picked it up, one on each side, and I went with him to reception because I was curious to see what Caridad's boyfriend looked like. But he had gone by the time we got there and I didn't feel like waiting for him to come back. The Peruvian and the receptionist noticed something odd about my behavior. According to the receptionist, Caridad's friend wouldn't be long, he must have been having a beer or choosing a campsite, but my instincts were telling me to make myself scarce. I went into the street and fell into step with the rest of the passersby, wondering if I'd run into Caridad in town, wondering if I'd have the strength to go out to the old mansion on the outskirts. When I got to the Paseo Marítimo, I tried to follow my previous route, walking alongside the gardens as I had done the day before. At the end of the esplanade where the hang gliders had been, a Catalan brass band was setting up. When I asked if the hang-gliding competition was over, the reply was affirmative. What happened to the last pilot? My interlocutor, an old man who was walking his little dog, shrugged his shoulders. They've all gone, he said. For a while I leaned against the trunk of a tree, with my back to the café terraces, listening to the band's first chords; then I left the Paseo and plunged into the streets of the port district. I recognized some bars from the night before. In a place with table soccer and video games, I thought I saw Caridad's black hair; but it wasn't her. I escaped from the bustle by walking up the streets that climb toward the church. Suddenly I found myself wandering on quiet sidewalks where the only sounds came from open windows and televisions. I went back down toward the waterfront via an avenue full of linden trees and badly parked cars. There wasn't the slightest breeze. Before I reached the first terrace, I heard Carmen's voice rising over the general racket. She seemed to be warming up, just for fun. I looked in at the door of a seedy bar in one of the streets coming off the Paseo, and there she was, sitting among the scattered clients, drinking a caffe latte and a glass of cognac. I ordered a beer and found a place next to her. She didn't recognize me at first, but when she did it was like she'd been expecting me. Hi, cutie, she said, I'm going to introduce you to a friend. Next to her was a small thin man of indefinite age—he could have been forty or sixty—with a large pear-shaped head, who held out his hand most politely. He was wearing baggy blue drill trousers and a yellow T-shirt. When we sat down again, after the formalities, Carmen announced that she would be beginning her performance any minute. I had the impression she was letting me know in case I wanted to leave, but I stayed put and said nothing. Then her companion spoke: Song is the best cure for summer heat, he said ceremoniously, in a tone of voice that seemed to betray both shyness and contentment. To reinforce his declaration he showed us his long rabbit-like teeth, stained with nicotine. Shut up, Rookie, you're always talking crap, Carmen said as she stood up and, after briefly clearing her throat, launched into a cabaret number, with her head and bust perfectly still, as if she had suffered a sudden seizure or been transformed into a statue from the waist up, her feet advancing cautiously on their stiletto heels, her fluttering hands both marking the rhythm and adroitly collecting the coins proferred by members of the audience. Her circuit was short, like the song, which garnered two or three weary-sounding compliments from people who seemed to know her repertoire. When she came back to us Carmen had three hundred pesetas in her hand, which she slammed down on the table like dominoes, next to her caffe latte and cognac, while bowing discreetly in the direction of the door, where there was no one to be seen.

Bravo! That's the way! said the Rookie, and gulped down the remainder of his drink, a Cuba Libre from the look of it. Hold the bullshit, shut your trap, replied the singer resonantly, flushed from her efforts. All her movements, her acknowledgement of the empty door, for example, seemed to be dictated by a sense of etiquette that left no room for improvisation, as if every bow and gaze complied with a code that the singer was obeying to the letter. The Rookie shifted contentedly in his seat and called for another Cuba Libre. Beside him, Carmen sipped her caffe latte while surreptitiously watching my hands. A wall clock surrounded by soccer banners showed the time: 9 p.m. With a haughty air, the waiter put another Cuba Libre on our table. That's the fucking way! whispered the Rookie, and knocked back three-quarters of the glass. Down with contempt, down with spite, he added. You've lost your bearings too, haven't you, cutie-locks? I asked what she meant by cutie-locks. The Rookie laughed very softly and tapped on the table with his knuckles and his fingertips. She's not going to come, said Carmen. Who's she? Caridad, who else? The singer and the Rookie looked at each other meaningfully. I have to go, I said. Off you go, boy, murmured the Rookie; his eyes were glassy and smiling, but he wasn't drunk. For a moment he seemed to be a doll, or a dwarf who had suddenly decided to grow. I didn't get up from my chair. I don't know how much time went by. I remember the sweat dripping from my face like rainwater, and at one point I looked at the Rookie and saw that his face, with its rugged, healthy-looking skin, was completely dry. The bar had filled up, and without any warning, Carmen got up and repeated her number. This time she seemed to sing a little more loudly, but I couldn't be sure; I thought it was louder, and sadder as well. I realize now that I didn't want to leave because I knew that once I got out into the street, I would have to choose between going back to start my shift and going on toward the outskirts of Z. In the end fear won out and I walked quickly back to the campground, as if someone was following me . . .

ENRIC ROSQUELLES:

How do you think I felt when I found out

How do you think I felt when I found out that there was something more than friendship between Nuria and Remo Morán? Terrible, I felt terrible. My world was falling apart and my spirit revolted against such a cruel injustice. I should say: the repetition of such an injustice, because some years before, in similar circumstances, I had seen Lola, my best social worker, an extremely efficient girl, enviably balanced and positive too, fall into the clutches of that South American dealer, who soon destroyed her life. Morán degraded, despoiled and defiled everything he touched. Lola is divorced now, and seems to be leading a normal life, but I know she's hurting inside, and maybe it will take her years to recover the glow of freshness and joy she had before that unfortunate encounter. No, I never liked Morán; I could never stomach him, as they say. I have a natural talent for judging people and right from the start I knew he was a fraud, a charlatan. Some have said I hated him because he was an artist. A con artist more like it! I adore art! Why would I have risked my position and my future to build the skating rink if I didn't? It was simply that he didn't fool me with that world-weary, seen-it-all manner of his. So he'd been through a war. So he'd been on TV a couple times. So his dick was a foot long. God almighty! I'm surrounded by a pack of rabid dogs! My former subordinates, despicable busybodies from Fairs and

Festivals, Child Welfare, the volunteers from Civil Defense, all the people affected by my budget cutbacks, who were shifted to smaller offices, or simply sacked because I didn't want dead wood in my departments, now they're trying to get their own back by making up stories, casting the Latino as the hero and me as the villain. Morán's a clown, he's never been near a war; he might have been on television, on some local show, but who hasn't these days; and let me tell you a secret I discovered a long time ago: size is not everything. What women really want from a man is affection and tenderness. Unless you think you need a foot-long tool to reach the clitoris? Or stimulate the G-spot? When I think of Lola walking along the beach, hand in hand with her little boy, to whom they gave some unfortunate Indian name I can never remember, I feel I have every reason to hate Morán. Yes, I tried to get rid of him, but always within the strict bounds of the law. I had seen him only three times in my life before the regrettable incidents at the Palacio Benvingut, and each time, if I'm not mistaken, he boasted about flouting the current regulations forbidding the employment of foreigners without work permits. As far as I know, Morán and the small-time farmers around Z were the only ones consciously breaking the law. With the market gardeners, or some of them at least, it was understandable if not excusable; the lettuces, for example, had to be harvested, and the pool of laborers available was basically made up of Africans, most of whom didn't have their papers in order. I don't like Africans. Especially if they're Muslims. Once, in passing, I suggested to my team in Social Services that we could gather up all the street kids in Z and give them jobs on the farms: sowing, harvesting, driving tractors, even working on the market stalls each morning. It would have been marvelous to see that generation of future delinquents and junkies working the land. Of course the idea was rejected, almost as if it had been a joke. I wasn't entirely convinced myself. A bit too much like slave labor, they said, bad for our image. We'll never know now. As I was saying, the farmers had their reasons. But Morán used to employ foreigners just to bug us! I once mentioned this in passing to Lola, when she was still his wife, and I still remember what she said. According to Lola, Morán used to hire old friends, friends he had made when he was eighteen, a bunch of poets who had eventually washed up in the Mother Country one way or another. He found them, or came across them, through a combination of luck and concern; he gave them work, helped (or forced) them to save, and at the end of the season they invariably went back to their respective places of origin in Latin America. Or that's what Morán told Lola, at least. She never made friends with any of them, although she judged them all to be worthy of her professional attention. Scruffy, damaged individuals; resentful, taciturn, sickly misfits, the sort you'd rather not encounter on a deserted street. I should say that in spite of the gulf between me and her husband, my professional relationship with Lola was, and I trust still is, founded on a sense of friendship and team spirit—after the mayor, she was my closest collaborator—and there was no reason to doubt what she confided in me. The aforesaid poets, completely unknown in Spain as indeed in Latin America, were never very numerous, and must have blended in with the rest of the motley staff, which comprised a range of characters to satisfy all tastes. I never saw any of them, and I only remember the story now because of the aftereffect it had on me, like a horror film. Anyway, as I put it to Lola, was he helping out his old friends and colleagues, or just trying to get rid of them? Lola pointed out that they might not all have gone back to Latin America, maybe they just didn't come back to Z, but the way their departures coincided with the end of the season struck me as too neat. Which raises another question: did they go back empty-handed, apart from the few pesetas they would have been able to save, or was the trip a way of continuing to work for Morán as couriers or messengers? It's well known that the drug trade is comfortably established in Z, and more than once I heard it said that Morán was involved, although to be honest I should add that the claims were unconfirmed. Of course I never mentioned any of this to Lola, out of respect more than anything; after all, Morán was the father of her child. Twice I called some acquaintances in Gerona to see if they had anything on him. But I drew a blank. People drop off the twig when they're ripe. Needless to say, the labor inspectors never got anywhere when they went to visit. I didn't have any illusions about that. I know exactly how those bureaucrats operate; they wouldn't have tried to take him by surprise by calling at an unexpected time, questioning all the staff, checking with the neighbors and so on. As long as they kept using their traditional methods, Morán was always going to slip through the net, without even a token fine. Another solution would have been to report him to the Trade Union Councils, but I don't have very good relations with the union officials in Z. Only once in my life have I been in a fight, about five or six years ago, when I encountered a group of maniacs at the entrance to the UGT headquarters. It was me and a municipal police-man, who has since retired, against eight or nine heavies from the strike committee. To be honest, there were so many of them I don't remember the exact number. Luckily the fight was brief, and there were more slaps and pushes than punches. All the same I came away with a bleeding nose and an eyebrow gashed open, and Pilar dropped whatever urgent task she was engaged in to come and see me straight away. It's strange: as a child, I never bullied anyone and no one bullied me; I had to come to Z and work like a slave and fall in love to get beaten up. I want to make it clear that I said nothing to Nuria; not a word of reproach or anything that could be taken as such. I stifled my rage and (why not admit it?) my jealousy and the utter shock of it all. Her body language and the way she brought up the subject made it clear to me that Nuria herself didn't entirely understand what was happening with Morán, and that my interference could only make things worse. The pain I felt did not reduce the intensity of my love, but transformed it continually, producing new mental pleasures. And I had plenty to keep me busy; my antagonism toward Remo Morán has never, thank God, represented more than three per cent of my emotional investment. Around that time I dreamed of the ice rink again. It was like the extension of an earlier dream: outside, the world was subjected to a temperature of 105 degrees in the shade, while inside the Palacio Benvingut, the glacial chill of the air was cracking the old mirrors. The dream began precisely when I put on the skates and went gliding, without the slightest effort, over the smooth white surface, whose purity, it seemed to me, was peerless. A deep and final silence enveloped everything. Suddenly, impelled by the force of my own skating, I left the rink, or what I thought was the rink, and began to skate through the corridors and rooms of the Palacio Benvingut. The machinery must have gone crazy, I thought, and coated the whole house in ice. Flying along at a dizzying speed, I reached the rooftop terrace, from which I could see a corner of the town and the electric pylons. They seemed to be overcharged, about to explode or stride away toward the coves. Further away I could see a small, almost black pine wood on a slope, and above it some red clouds like slightly open duck bills. Duck bills with shark's teeth! Nuria's bike appeared, moving very slowly along the dirt road, just as huge flames erupted from Z. The glow lasted only a few seconds, then the whole horizon was plunged in darkness. I'm done for, I thought, it's a blackout. I woke as the ice beneath my feet was beginning to melt at an alarming rate. This dream reminded me of a book I had read as a teenager. The author of the book (whose name I have forgotten) claims to be recounting some kind of legend about the struggle between good and evil. Evil and its agents establish the empire of fire on earth. They spread, make war and are invincible. In the final, crucial battle, good unleashes ice upon the armies of evil and brings them to a halt. Gradually the fire is extinguished and vanishes from the face of the earth. It ceases to be a danger. The agents of good are victorious at last. Nevertheless, the legend warns that the struggle will soon begin again since hell is inexhaustible. When the ice began to melt, that was exactly the feeling I had: along with the Palacio Benvingut, I was plummeting into hell . . .

REMO MORÁN:

I decided to go and look for Nuria at her place

I decided to go and look for Nuria at her place, something I had never done, and that was how I met her mother and her sister, a very clever little girl called Laia. The sun was beating down that afternoon, but there were plenty of people out walking in the streets, which were full of food vendors and ice cream stands, and all kinds of merchandise, which the storekeepers had spread out almost to the edge of the sidewalk. A slim woman, slightly shorter than Nuria, opened the door and invited me in, just like that, as if she had been expecting me for a long time. Nuria wasn't home. I tried to leave, but it was too late; politely but firmly, the woman blocked the exit. I soon realized that she wanted to pump me for information about her daughter. I was corralled into the living room, where there were trophies on little fake-marble pedestals. Photos and press cuttings in aluminum frames hung on both sides of the chimney, proclaiming former triumphs. They showed Nuria skating on her own or with others; some of the cuttings were in English, French and something that might have been Danish or Swedish. My daughter has been skating since she was six years old, announced the woman, standing in a doorway that led through to a spacious kitchen with the blinds down, which gave it the look of a dim wood, a clearing in a wood at midnight. In the living room, a pleasant yellow light was filtering through the curtains. Have you seen my girl skate? she asked in Catalan, but before I could answer she repeated the question in Spanish. I said no, I had never seen her skate. She stared at me in disbelief. Her eyes were as blue as Nuria's, but without the glint of iron will. I accepted a cup of coffee. A monotonous, repetitive sound was coming from the back of the house; my first thought, absurdly, was that someone must have been splitting firewood. Are you South American? asked Nuria's mother, sitting down in an armchair patterned with sepia flowers against a grey background. I replied in the affirmative. Would Nuria be long? You never know with Nuria, she said, looking at a bag from which knitting needles and balls of wool were protruding. I lied about another engagement, although I knew it wouldn't be so easy to get away. What country are you from? Argentina? Although her smile was fairly neutral, it seemed to be giving me little taps on the back, inviting me to bare my soul. I told her I was Chilean. Ah, I see, from Chile, she said. And what do you do? I have a jewelry store, I mumbled. Here, in Z? I nodded, going along with everything. How odd, she said, Nuria has never mentioned you. The coffee was scalding but I drank it quickly; someone squealed behind me, and from the corner of my eye I saw a shadow slip into the kitchen. Nuria's mother said, Come here, I want to introduce you to one of Nuria's friends. The little Martí girl appeared before me, holding a can of Coca-Cola. We shook hands and smiled. Laia sat down beside her mother, separated from her only by the bag of wool, and waited; I remember she was wearing shorts and sporting large purple scabs on both knees. My husband saw her skate only once, but he died happy, said Nuria's mother. I looked at her in utter bewilderment. For a moment I thought she was telling me that her husband had died *while* watching Nuria skate, but to ask for an explanation would have been even more absurd than my initial supposition, so all I did was nod. He died in the hospital, said Laia, and went on staring at me as she sipped her Coca-Cola with chilling parsimony. In room 304 of the Z hospital, she specified. Mrs Martí looked at her with an admiring smile. Another coffee, Mr Morán? I said no, it was delicious, but no thanks. Strangely, I had the impression that the decision to go or stay was no longer mine to make. Do you know what Nuria is doing here? I thought Laia was referring to the real flesh-and-blood Nuria, and spun around, startled, only to find an empty corridor behind me. Laia's index finger was pointing at one of the framed photographs. I confessed my ignorance and laughed. Nuria's mother laughed with me, understandingly. What an idiot I am, I said, I thought Nuria was behind me. This is a "loop," said Laia, a "loop." And do you know what she's doing here? The photo had been taken from a distance, to show the size of the rink and the stands; in the middle, leaning slightly to the right, a shorter-haired Nuria had been frozen on the point of taking illusory flight. This is a "bracket," said Laia. And this is the end of a series of "threes." And that's the "Catalan" figure, invented by a Catalan skater. Having expressed my admiration, I examined the photographs one by one. In some of them, Nuria was no more than ten or twelve years old; her legs were like matchsticks and she looked very thin. In others she was skating arm in arm with a muscular, long-haired boy, and they were smiling demonstratively: gleaming teeth, a focused look, but all the same they did seem genuinely happy. Overwhelmed by the whirl of photos, I suddenly felt tired and sad. When will Nuria be back? I asked. There was a plaintive sound to my voice. Later on, after training, said Laia. I hadn't noticed her mother reach for the needles, but now she was knitting with a contented look on her face, as if she had found out all she needed to know. Training? In Barcelona? Laia smiled confidentially: No, in Z, skating or jogging or playing tennis. Skating? Like I said, *skating*, Laia replied. She always comes home late. And then, after checking that her mother wasn't paying attention, she whispered in my ear: With Enric. Ah, I sighed. Do you know Enric? asked Laia. I said yes, I knew him. So she trains with Enric every day? Every day! shouted Laia. Even Sunday . . .

GASPAR HEREDIA:

I'm a rookie in this hell-hole of a town, said the Rookie

I'm a rookie in this hell-hole of a town, said the Rookie when I asked him how he got his name. A rookie, a newbie at the age of forty-eight, a hick who doesn't know his way around the traps, and has no friends to help him out. He earned a bit of money salvaging stuff from dumpsters, and spent the rest of the day hanging around bars away from the beach, on the edges of Z, where the tourists don't go, or clinging like a limpet to the ever-unpredictable Carmen. She had dubbed him the Rookie, and it sounded best coming from her: Rookie, do this; Rookie, do that; Tell me your woes, Rookie; Time for a drink, Rookie. When Carmen said "Rookie," you could hear the background music of an Andalusian street, full of poor draftees on leave, looking for a cheap rooming house or a train to save them from the disaster foreseen in recurring dreams. Her lazy, luminous intonation, which, by the way, made the Rookie swoon with delight, had something of the men's shower room about it, with a little hole in the roof for the Field Marshall's young daughter to peep through each morning and see the soldiers suffering under the cold showers. Right then, a cold shower was a tempting thought—the air was thick with heat, and for hours at a time it was hard to do more than feel resentful and gasp for breath—but the cold shower in Carmen's voice was terrible. Terrible, yes, but desirable, and systematically marvelous. The Rookie worked the dumpsters, or scavenged cardboard boxes directly from shops and warehouses; then he sold his stock to Z's one and only recycler, a greedy little son of a bitch, and that was the end of his working day. He tried to spend the rest of his time with Carmen, though he didn't always succeed. It was, incidentally, his first visit to Z, although his friendship with the singer dated back to their meeting in Barcelona, a year or two before. She's the reason I washed up in this heartless town, he explained to whoever would listen. I came here one stormy night, my friend, following that fickle woman, and often she won't even spend the night with me. To which Carmen replied that she valued nothing more highly than her independence; the Rookie, she felt, should emulate the forbearance of the Catalans, the civilized practice of biding one's time. Don't you know there are things we're not meant to know, Rookie? Don't you know it's crass to ask too many questions? The Rookie moved his head and hands in desperate assent, but he was clearly not convinced by the singer's explanations. His greatest fear was that a separation, however short, would lead to death, a sudden death for both of them one night. The worst thing about dying alone, he used to say, is not being able to say good-bye. And why would you want to say good-bye when you're dying, Rookie? Better to think of the people you love and say good-bye to them in your imagination. They often talked about death, sometimes in a quarrelsome way, although mostly they seemed to be either detached, as if the subject was of no personal concern to them, or phlegmatic, as if the worst was already well and truly over. The only real source of conflict—from time to time—was the business of sleeping alone. The Rookie wanted to sleep with Carmen every night, and when she refused, he was clearly suspicious and felt abandoned and cross. Their friendship had been born in a homeless shelter and was still going strong, they affirmed triumphantly. You can't compare living things, you see, said Carmen. Take plants, for example, they're happy with a thimbleful of water, or take the trees called oaks or the ones they call stone pines: they might be engulfed by the flames of a forest fire, or brought back to life by a trickle of dirty pee . . . to which the Rookie replied that he was happy with something to eat and shelter from the cold. Dreamily, maybe remembering *Lady and the Tramp*, the singer said that the Rookie was a hick and she was a lady of quality, that's just the way it was. To bridge the gap, perhaps, they had taken to telling stories, and sometimes they would spend hours going over their pasts; the way they talked you might have thought they had known each other from the age of five and witnessed every episode in both their lives. They were confident about the future: Spain is on the path to glory, they used to say. And about their personal futures. Everything was going to work out; when autumn came, they wouldn't have to leave Z, not even when winter came. On the contrary, they would have a good house with a fireplace or an electric heater to keep them warm and a television to keep them entertained, and the Rookie's patience would pay off, he'd find work, not some boring or backbreaking job— their days of slave labor were over—no, something stable, like cleaning the windows of offices and restaurants, or guarding empty apartment buildings, or gardening for the local fat cats in their big houses, although for that he'd need a car and proper tools. The Rookie's eyes opened wide when Carmen conjured that rosy future. And what will you do, Carmen? I'll give singing lessons, I'll train young voices, and take it nice and easy. That's the fucking way! That's what I like about women: the up and down! Everything that goes up comes down and whatever hits the bottom rises back up to the surface again, exclaimed the Rookie fervently. I have a plan, Carmen confessed to me, but my lips are sealed, it's a secret I'd guard with my life. Yet temptation overcame her prudent resolve, or she simply forgot that she wasn't supposed to tell, and one afternoon she explained, in broad outline, her plan to us: first of all she would go and put herself on the electoral roll in Z, then she'd pay a visit to the mayor's henchman, and ask for, no, demand, a public housing apartment, and thirty years to pay it off; then, to drive her point home, she'd tell him a few things to prove the reliability of her sources, or, if he preferred, she'd and go tell the mayor—it would be up to him. And how do you know who Madame Mayor's henchman is? asked the Rookie. From experience, said the singer, and, running a green comb through her hair, she began to tell us what had happened during a previous stay in Z, two or three years before, she wasn't sure exactly, maybe even four years ago, but she did remember her daily visits to City Hall trying to get some help. Purgatory. At the time Carmen had thought she was critically ill and she was scared. Scared of dying alone and abandoned, as the Rookie said. But she didn't die. That was how I got to know all those bureaucratic vermin. The jackals and the vultures. Dyed-in-the-wool liberals quite prepared to let me die, without showing any pity or even laughing when I cracked a joke or imitated Montserrat Caballé for them. Never trust anyone who works in an office, cutie. Assholes, the lot of them; they will all be put to the sword, one way or another. There was just one girl who really tried to help me: the social worker, a very pretty girl, and she knew her classics backwards and forwards too. Opera classics, that is. That's how I got to know the mayor's henchman, I mean how I got to know what he's like inside:

blacker than a hole. It was like this: I kept demanding an appointment with the mayor, and eventually her secretary sent me to see the henchman, who sent me to see the social worker. The girl would have solved my problem but they didn't let her. I know because I used to hang around outside the offices of Child Welfare and Social Services each morning, mainly because so-called working hours aren't much good for singing, and the waiting room was air conditioned. I adore air conditioning, cutie. Well, that was where I heard the henchman through an office door, sounding like Zeus himself, thundering against all sorts of things in general and me in particular. I wasn't registered to vote in Z, and that was a mortal sin, never to be redeemed. I don't have official proof of identity, just a Caritas card and my Red Cross donor's card, so you see the bind I was in. I'm not registered to vote anywhere. But even the police, when they stop me in the street, know they should turn a blind eye to such things. In the end I got better on my own and didn't need his help any more. When health returns to the body, you cheer up and forget, but I haven't forgotten that wretch's face. The shoe is on the other foot now; I happen to have come by some information (from a perfectly sound and reliable source) and I'm going to demand whatever I feel like. Not a hospital bed but an apartment, and some help to start a new life; it's payback time. She wouldn't say what sort of information she had come by. It sounded very much like blackmail but it was hard to imagine Carmen in the role of blackmailer. The Rookie suggested she ask for a camper instead of an apartment, that way they could go from place to place. No, an apartment, said the singer, an apartment and thirty years to pay it off. We laughed and talked about apartments for quite a while, until it occurred to me to ask how Caridad fitted into all this. Caridad is a very clever girl, said the singer with a wink, though at the moment she's a bit poorly, so I'm taking care of her; when I get the apartment, she can come and live with me. You're as generous as the sun, said the Rookie with a touch of envy. After me, they broke the mold, said Carmen. And if they ignore you, what will you do? If who ignores me, cutie? The people at City Hall, the mayor's man, everyone . . . Carmen burst out laughing, her teeth were chipped and uneven, and most of her molars were gone, but her jaw, by contrast, was strong and well-formed, the sort that holds firm when things are falling apart. You don't know what I have on them, she said, you don't know what a fuss I'm prepared to kick up. You and Caridad? Me and Caridad, said the singer, two heads are better than one . . .

ENRIC ROSQUELLES:

I am used to being the object of resentful gazes

I am used to being the object of resentful gazes, but it was only that summer, my last summer in Z, that I began to notice something else in the way people were looking at me, a mixture of malice and anticipation. At first I presumed it was because of the approaching elections; there were quite a few people on the City Council who had spent the previous four years waiting to see Pilar defeated, and me with her. I was slow to realize that this time it was different; the council employees who still hadn't gone on vacation seemed physically rather than mentally possessed by a kind of unspoken suspicion. I tried to be pleasant but it was no use; their gazes remained fixed on the windows or the tables, the washbasins or the stairs. Not one disrespectful remark or barbed joke was uttered in my presence, yet I couldn't help feeling that I was being condemned. In the end, as always, I put it all down to stress, the crazy hours I was working and my private problems, because, after all, no one had said anything that could be construed as criticism, and the usual sycophants went on congratulating me whenever one of my undertakings came to fruition. Even the projects that withered away, to stick to botanical metaphors, met with an appreciative response, a consoling remark of some sort: the town's governance would need to develop before such an initiative could make its mark, and so on. The fact is that I lowered my guard, and those signs, which could have saved me so much grief had I been able to read them correctly, passed me by, leaving only a vague sense of persecution, to which I was in any case accustomed. At the time Pilar had just come back from a trip to Mallorca, partly work, partly a vacation, during which one of the party's big wheels had suggested, half in earnest, half in jest—in keeping with the dominant mood in Mallorca at the time—that she could have a significant role to play in the Catalan parliament. Pilar, needless to say, returned to Z in a state of high excitement, and was constantly on the phone to people in Barcelona, the few who had stayed in the city or had come back already from their vacations, which is to say very few indeed, but that did not prevent her from getting a head start and sounding out, as they say, a number of well-placed and influential friends. I realize now that her febrile excitement worked in my favor, but it also allowed me to relax my vigilance, and that was to cost me dearly in the long run. Some advice for beginners: never drop your guard. Pilar, my nervous indecisive Pilar, needed to talk to someone she could trust, and as usual I was the one she chose. She was facing a moral dilemma: should she stand for re-election as mayor, knowing that in a few months' time she would have to resign? Would her supporters feel snubbed when she took up a seat in the regional parliament? Or would they understand that, in her new position, she would be better placed to defend the interests of Z? We considered the problem from various points of view, and when I had convinced her that there was in fact no moral dilemma, she felt confident about the future, as she put it. So confident that she invited a few friends from her inner circle to celebrate in advance as it were, at Z's best restaurant, which specializes in seafood and is one of the priciest places on the Costa Brava. And that's where I made my second mistake; it was understandable, but I will never forgive myself. I took Nuria to the dinner. What a night of dizzy joy it was! A night full of stars and tears and music strewn over the sea. I can still see the looks on their faces when they saw me turn up arm in arm with Nuria! There were four couples: the mayor and her husband, the councilors in charge of culture and tourism with their respective wives, and the surprise couple, Nuria and myself. It all went smoothly at the start. Enric, the mayor's husband, was particularly cheerful and sparky. A cynic might have attributed his good mood to the prospect of Pilar spending a lot of time away in Barcelona. It was a pleasure to listen to him, truly it was. Normally I can't stand a raconteur, but Enric's an exception. Before the entrées arrived, he had us all in stitches, treating us to mischievous anecdotes about various apparently idiotic acquaintances and even friends. Enric Gibert's reputation in Z as an intellectual and a man of the world is well deserved. Normally he's a serious and reserved person, but a celebration is a celebration. Maybe Nuria's presence helped to unfetter his wit, I don't know, but faced with her beauty there were only two options: to remain silent throughout the evening or to be an intelligent, vivacious, dazzling conversationalist. I have no doubt that Pilar was glad when she saw us walk in together. Nuria's beauty was like a prefiguration or a symbol of her triumph, but apart from that, I know that my happiness, the happiness of her faithful lieutenant, made her happy too; ingratitude is not one of Pilar's faults, and, as I have said already, she had every good reason to be grateful to me. With the arrival of the entrée, Z's traditional fisherman's soup, the mayor's husband was briefly upstaged: the owner's nephew came over to the table with two bottles of wine from the special reserve and took the opportunity to ask Pilar how her vacation in Mallorca had gone. Pilar and he are the same age, and I think they were even at school together. The owner's nephew is one of the most active members of the Convergencia i Unión party in Z, but that didn't prevent him from being on frank and friendly terms with Pilar. Until recently, political rivalry was civilized in Z; after the scandal, of course, they cast aside all propriety and revealed their true, bestial natures, but at the time our social interactions were still governed by common sense. Those were, in fact, the last days of common sense. Or to be exact, the last hours . . .

Remo Morán

The days that preceded the discovery of the body

The days that preceded the discovery of the body were un-
deniably strange: freshly painted inside and out, and silent,
as if we could somehow all sense the imminence of a ca-
lamity. I remember during my second year in Z, the body
of a teenage girl, almost a child, was found in a vacant lot;
she'd been killed and raped. The killer was never found.
Around that time there was a series of murders, all fitting
the same pattern; they began in Tarragona and moved up
the coast, leaving a trail of bodies (girls killed and raped,
in that order) all the way to Port Bou, as if the killer was
a tourist on the way home, but a very leisurely tourist, because a whole summer season elapsed between the first and
the last of the crimes. That was a good summer for business. We made money, and there still wasn't much competition. As you would expect, the police found some of the
culprits: screwed-up kids, office workers who had always
led quiet, irreproachable lives, a German truck driver, and
even, in the most widely publicized case, a policeman. But
at least three of the crimes remained unsolved, including
the one in Z. I remember that on the day the body was
discovered (the girl, I mean, not the body I found), before I
heard anything about it, I felt that something bad had happened in the town. The streets were luminous, as the streets
of childhood sometimes seem in memory, and although
we were having a hot summer the morning was cool, and

had the feel of something freshly made, an impression that extended to the houses, the washed-down sidewalks, and the faint but clearly recognizable sounds. Then I heard the news and soon it was the topic of every conversation. The mystery, the sense of suspended reality, gradually dissipated. In just the same way, the four or five days before I found the body were atypical days, not a succession of fragments and hours, but solid blocks dominated by a single unrelenting light: the will to persist whatever the cost, unhearing, unseeing, without the slightest groan of protest. The feeling was no doubt intensified by Nuria's absence, which left me dejected and anxious, and by the almost certain knowledge that, whatever I did, my relationship with her was condemned to failure. I think it was only then that I realized how much I had come to love her. But the realization didn't help. On the contrary. When I think of those afternoons now, it makes me laugh, but I wasn't laughing at the time, and even now, there's often something strained about my laughter. I listened to Loquillo, especially the sad songs, and hardly left my room or the triangle formed by my room, the hotel bar and a bar near the campground that was being run that season by a Dutch guy and a Spanish girl who were friends of Alex's. But drinking in a seaside town buzzing with tourists isn't really drinking. It only gives you a headache. I longed for the bars of Barcelona or Mexico City, but I knew that those places, those perfect dives, had vanished forever. And maybe that's why, a couple of times, I went to the campground looking for Gasparín. I never found him. The second time I went, the receptionist informed me, though no one had asked her opinion, that my friend was an odd boy (a boy!), and that as far as she could tell he hadn't slept for a couple of weeks. On more than one occasion she had gone to fetch him, so he could give them a hand, since they were short-staffed on the day shift. But his tent was always empty. She had only seen him about three times since he started work, and that wasn't normal. I tried to reassure her by explaining that he was a poet; she replied that her boyfriend, the Peruvian, was a poet too, but he didn't behave like that. Like a zombie. I didn't feel like arguing with her. Especially when, examining her fingernails, she remarked that poetry was a waste of time. She was right; on the planet of happy eunuchs and zombies, poetry is a waste of time. These days she's living with the Peruvian, and although I couldn't make it to the wedding, I sent them a state-of-the-art pressure cooker. That was Lola's suggestion; we sometimes go shopping together for our son, although it's really an excuse for a coffee and a chat somewhere in downtown Gerona. In the end it was better that I didn't find Gasparín, because my reason for wanting to see him was totally selfish: I wanted to talk, pour out my soul, and reminisce, with a little help from a friend, about the golden streets we had trodden together in the old days (the *good* old days), but in fact that was all just a way of skirting around what was, for me, the real issue: Nuria transformed into a series of images that had nothing to do with the girl I know. For my dark purposes a sports aficionado would have been more useful, but the only person I could think of was the barber, José, and he knew nothing about figure skating anyway. So in the end I had no one to talk to, which was just as well; it forced me to let the time go by in a more dignified manner. I think I said this already, but I'll say it again just in case: it wasn't the first time I'd seen a corpse. It had happened twice before. The first time was in Chile, in Concepción, the capital of the south. I was looking out the big window of the gymnasium where I was imprisoned along with about a hundred other people: it was a November night in 1973, the moon was full, and in the courtyard I saw a fat guy surrounded by a ring of police detectives. They were all beating him with their fists, their feet, and rubber truncheons. After a while, the fat guy stopped protesting. Then he fell face down on the ground and it was only then that I realized he was barefoot. One of the detectives lifted his head by the hair and examined it for a moment. Another one said he must be dead. A third remembered having heard something about the fat guy having heart problems. They dragged him away by the feet. In the gymnasium just me and one other prisoner had witnessed the scene; the rest were bundled up sleeping wherever they could find a place, and the air was so thick with snores and sighs I thought we were going to suffocate. I came across the second dead body in Mexico, on the outskirts of Nogales, a city in the north. I was traveling with two friends, in a car that belonged to one of them, and we were going to meet two girls, who in the end never turned up. Before we got to the meeting place, I got out to urinate and probably wandered too far from the highway. The body was between two humps of orange-colored earth, face up, arms outstretched, with a small hole in the forehead, just above the nose; it looked like it could have been made by a hole-punch, although it had in fact been made by a bullet, a .22. A faggot's gun, said one of my friends. The other friend was Gasparín; he took a look at the body but didn't say anything. Sometimes in the mornings, when I'm having breakfast on my own, I think I would have loved to be a detective. I'm pretty observant, and I can reason deductively, and I'm a keen reader of crime fiction. If that's any use . . . which it isn't . . . Anyway, as Hans Henny Jahn, I think, once wrote: if you find a murder victim, better brace yourself, because the bodies will soon be coming thick and fast . . .

GASPAR HEREDIA:

I watched Carmen and the Rookie from a distance

I watched Carmen and the Rookie from a distance: they were on the beach, gesturing wildly, lunging at each other and dodging; their feints were more like a hieroglyphic script than acts of aggression. Meanwhile, the swimmers, ignoring their quarrel, were heading back to their hotels, leaving them alone, enveloped in a veil of spray. Then, suddenly, Carmen left the beach and set off along the Paseo. The Rookie turned around, and after a moment of hesitation, sat down on the sand. From where I was, he looked like a dark mossy rock that had turned up on the beach the night before. I didn't stop for long. Two hundred yards ahead of me, I could hear Carmen's voice (it was impossible to see her in the thick mass of tourists) singing, "I am a shepherdess in Arcadia." Mistakenly, I thought she had stopped and that if I kept walking, I was bound to catch up with her. For a long time, guided only by her song, I followed Carmen along the Paseo Marítimo, until I reached the Esplanade. Gradually I slowed my pace to match hers, the leisurely pace of a queen returning to her castle. Now she was singing, "I am a wounded thrush at the gates of Hell," and in the faces of the people coming the other way, in some of those faces at least, I could see little sneers or empty smiles, flickers that bore unequivocal witness to Carmen's passage and her terrifying energy. I won't go into the details of how I shadowed her. It was more or less like the first time I followed Caridad. The streets were different and the pace was slower, but the destination was the same: the old mansion on the outskirts of Z. Carmen, as I noticed when we left town and set off on the highway that runs alongside the sea, was drunk. She would stop every ten paces and pull a bottle from her bag, then, a moment later, after taking a swig or two, resume her increasingly erratic and unsteady journey. I could hear her voice in snatches, carried by the evening breeze curling around the rocks, emphatically intoning, "I am a bell in the snow, tudum, tudum" almost as if it was a hymn. Just before reaching the mansion, I let her get ahead and stopped to think. What was I doing there? Did I really want to find Caridad, whatever the consequences might be? And if I did find her, what would I say? Would I have the courage to explain what I felt for her? I stayed there thinking for a good while, as cars sped recklessly around the bend in the highway, heading for Z or Y. Finally I got up and walked down the private road, still confused about what I wanted and what I felt. Curiosity was drawing me on, the desire to see the skating rink again, and the vague sense that I had to protect Caridad and the singer. As soon as I crossed the threshold of the mansion, the sound of the "Fire Dance" put an end to my ruminations. From then on it was like I was drugged. From then on the world was entirely transformed, and my fears and suspicions shrank away, obliterated by the brilliant alliance of desire and risk within those sturdy old walls. The fat guy was standing beside the rink, holding a notebook and a fountain pen. The arrangement of the packing cases had changed significantly since my last visit, so to get a good view of the whole rink without being seen I had to creep along the wall toward the generator. You're losing energy, said the fat guy, barely moving his lips.

The skater appeared like a breath of air from a corner of the rink beyond my field of vision and disappeared again immediately. There was something about their imperturbable presence in that abandoned mansion that reminded me of Carmen and the Rookie arguing on the beach. Did you hear me? said the fat guy. You're losing energy. The skater stopped on the edge of the rink, next to him, and without moving, or rather moving only her hips and her pelvis, performed a little dance that clearly had nothing to do with Manuel de Falla's music. The fat guy's lips relaxed beatifically. After this brief interlude, the skater bent down and resumed her exercises without saying a word. The fat guy turned his attention back to his notebook: Well, well, he said after a while. Do you know how much the folk dancing is going to cost this year? No, and I don't care, shouted the skater. The fat guy moved his head several times, nodding and shaking, and in between the nods and shakes he pursed his lips as if he was about to whistle or kiss someone on the cheek. I don't know, there was something about the guy that made him likeable. The rectangular rink seemed to be more brightly illuminated than last time and the humming of the generator, or generators, was louder, as if the machine was signaling that it had reached its maximum capacity. What a stupid waste of money, murmured the fat guy. The girl threw him a sidelong glance as she went past, then looked up at the beams from which the spotlights were hanging, and closed her eyes. Skating blind, she slowed down gradually, but also began to move in a more complex and confident way. Each turn and shift of position had clearly been practiced many times over. Finally she headed for the center of the rink, where she leaped up and span around several times before landing precisely and skating away. Bravo, whispered the fat guy. All I know about skating is what I learned from watching some Holiday on Ice show in a bar, but what she was doing seemed perfect to me. The skater continued with her eyes closed and tried to repeat the last maneuver. But what should have been a stylized T figure, her body outstretched horizontally, balanced on one vertical leg, as she sliced the rink into two equal halves, became a tumble of legs and arms that finished with her lying face up on the ice. Just then, at the opposite end of the rink, I saw Caridad's silhouette, hidden among the cases, like me. Have you hurt yourself? asked the fat guy, who started to walk onto the ice but then stopped. No, said the girl without trying to get up, her arms outstretched, her legs slightly apart and her hair spread like a cushion between her head and the ice. From the look on her face she didn't seem to be in pain or even upset about messing up the routine. But my attention was divided between the skater and the silhouette at the other end of the rink, which, to my horror, for a moment resembled the shadow of a huge, emaciated rat. Why don't you get up? Are you OK? Standing on tiptoe at the edge of the rink, the fat guy was clearly alarmed in the extreme. I'm fine, really, you shouldn't talk so much, it breaks my concentration, said the skater flat out on the ice. Talk? I hardly said a thing, replied the fat guy. What about those papers you were reading aloud? That's for my work, Nuria, don't be so touchy, he whined, anyway, I wasn't reading them out loud. Yes you were. A few comments, maybe, that was all, come on, Nuria, get up, you could damage your back lying there, said the fat guy. Why? Because it's very cold! Come here, help me up, said the skater. What? The fat guy put on an apologetic smile. The girl kept lying there quietly, waiting. Do you want me to help you? Don't you feel well? Have you hurt yourself, Nuria? The fat guy's body teetered precariously on the edge of the rink. There was something pendulum-like about him. Something uncannily reminiscent of a clockwork mechanism. Down at the other end, Caridad's whole head was visible over the cases. Come and lie down beside me, it's not that cold, said the skater. What do you mean not that cold? I swear, said the skater. The fat guy turned around. Caridad's head disappeared immediately. Had they seen her? Come on, stop playing around and get on with your training, said the fat guy after scrutinizing the darkness. The skater didn't answer. The spiky hair of the girl with the knife appeared again over the tops of the boxes. I figured the fat guy probably hadn't seen her, although from the way he had turned around, he was definitely expecting to find something behind him. Come here, said the skater, don't be afraid. You come here, replied the fat guy, in a barely audible voice. Still looking up at the roof, the skater smiled broadly and said, Chook chook chook. The fat guy heaved an exasperated sigh, walked around the chair and sat in it with his back to the skater, pointedly facing the rows of cases. Ignoring his body language, the girl sat up on the ice. What time is it? The fat guy looked at his watch and said something I couldn't hear. It's not a big deal, just a fall or two, you always exaggerate, said the skater. Maybe, said the fat guy, with irritation and affection in his voice, but so do you. Ever since I was a little girl, she confirmed. The fat guy stood up, looking happy, and said, Listen, I'm not your trainer but I know that lying on ice after skating has got to be bad for you. You've perspired and now you're getting cold. I know, I'm a silly girl, said the skater. I'm serious, Nuria, said the fat guy. Then they were quiet for a moment, observing each other, the girl in the middle of the rink, the fat guy perched on the cement edge, balancing on tiptoe with his hands in his pockets. Suddenly the skater was possessed by laughter. I'd like to see you skate, she sputtered between convulsions. Her laughter was sudden and cold like the ice. Yes, very funny, I'd fall over, said the fat guy. That's what I was thinking, but you could take the knocks, and I'd make you skate eight hours a day, until you fell asleep on your skates. I don't think you'd be that cruel, said the fat guy. What kind of dress could you wear? I know, a blue one, with flounces— and I would be that cruel, you don't know me. The fat guy nodded and pretended to get angry, but now and then let out a laugh, as if it had risen irrepressibly from deep inside. One day I'll skate, for you . . . he whispered. You couldn't, said the skater. I promise you I will, Nuria. The fat guy moved his left hand strangely, like a sleepwalker or someone opening a door. Sitting on the ice, no longer laughing, the skater observed him attentively, waiting for a declaration, but the fat guy said nothing more. Suddenly the skater hiccuped. What was that? said the fat guy, looking everywhere except the rink. Shit, I've got hiccups, said the skater. You see, I warned you, why don't you get up? It's from laughing so much, it's your fault, said the skater. Come on, I'll give you a glass of water and it'll go away, said the fat guy. That doesn't work with me, you're going to make me drink it backwards, aren't you? The fat guy looked at her admiringly. That what my grandma used to do, I almost broke my teeth once. They waited for the next hiccup in silence; even the "Fire Dance" seemed to be playing more quietly. At the other end of the rink, Caridad's silhouette rose above the cases until her head and shoulders were dimly visible. She was thinner than she had been at the campground, and the background of shadows and straight edges accentuated the impression of thinness. The skater's hiccup resonated in every corner. Well, it's always worked for me, said the fat guy. That's because you're so cautious, you'd never bite the glass and break a tooth, said the skater. You just put your lips on the edge, that's all. Do you want to see my method? The fat guy remained perfectly still, as if he had seen a lion in the middle of the rink, and then he tried to shake his head to say no, but it was too late. She had already clicked the blades of her skates together and was gliding over the ice towards him. When she got there, he was waiting, tremulous and attentive, with an enormous towel. You're cold, he said, let me rub you a bit. Turn off the tape, said the skater. The fat guy draped the towel over the girls' shoulders and promptly obeyed her order . . .

Enric Rosquelles:

Unfortunately, after dinner, Pilar insisted that we go to a disco

Unfortunately, after dinner, Pilar insisted that we go to a disco; she suddenly felt like dancing with her husband, something they hadn't done for a long time, and everyone thought it was a wonderful idea. Except me. I should have grabbed Nuria and made my getaway right then, but I thought she deserved a bit of fun. My big mistake, of course, was not foreseeing that someone would bring up the subject of skating. Nuria's presence, as I soon realized, made it inevitable, and the dreaded moment came while we were watching people make fools of themselves on the dance floor, before we had dared to do likewise. The councilor in charge of culture, or his wife, one of them, opened fire by asking if there was a competition coming up. Nuria's reply was utterly naïve: Yes. Initially there was some talk about her representing Z: she had to fly the flag and fly it high. Then, for want of a better topic, I guess, the difficulties and delicacy of skating were discussed (Like an iron butterfly, shouted out the councilor responsible for tourism, visibly pleased with his simile) and Nuria had no choice but to agree and assure them, with all her candid enthusiasm (poor Nuria), that she was training for at least five hours a day. In Barcelona? asked Enric Gibert. No, in Z, said Nuria, as emphatically as a tombstone being dropped into place on a grave. My grave. Luckily I have quick reflexes: right away I asked her to dance. As we walked away toward the dance floor, I looked back and saw Pilar staring at me. The rest of them were laughing and talking, but Pilar, who might be careless and negligent at times, but is certainly nobody's fool, kept her dark gimlet eyes fixed on me. I would gladly have kept on walking and never returned to that table. I was sweating, but not from the exertion. Dancing has never been my forte, but I threw myself into that alien world, perhaps to delay the impending catastrophe, albeit momentarily, perhaps to enjoy being close to Nuria for the last time. And to be honest, I wasn't too bad. All my usual fears vanished in the commotion of the dance floor, and I believe I can explain why: to dance well you have to forget your own body. It must cease to exist. In spite of all its extra pounds and its divergence from current esthetic norms, my body swayed and bounced, lifted one leg, then the other, then a leg and an arm, then leaped in the air and spun around, all without any help from my mind, which had, meanwhile, withdrawn to somewhere behind my eyeballs, where it was assessing the situation, weighing up the pros and cons, attempting to read Pilar's thoughts telepathically (with a certain trepidation, I admit), guessing at the scope of the questions she would ask and trying to fabricate convincing replies. When we came back to the table, we were literally dripping with perspiration. The wives of both councilors felt obliged to make humorous remarks about my little-known passion for dancing, which they summed up by saying, You've been keeping *that* quiet! I accepted their praise and their jokes good humouredly, since they were giving me a few seconds' grace. Pilar, by contrast, was not at all talkative; her husband had just gone to the bathroom. Inspired by my example, the councilors and their wives got up to dance, leaving only myself, Pilar and Nuria at the table, which was plunged in an ominous darkness. I remember there was a slow tune playing—was it a bolero?—and all the dancers who a moment before had been jumping around among the lights let their shoulders droop, went suddenly languid and collapsed into each other's arms. Wretched as I was, I thanked heaven that we were no longer dancing, since I was mortified by the thought of Nuria resting her head against my shoulder or my chest (as all the girls were doing, even the councilors' wives) and smelling the reek of my sweat. That's the way I am; I always try to make a good impression. No doubt people are saying now that on such-and-such an occasion my socks or my breath stank. Lies. In matters of personal hygiene I have always been scrupulous to a fault, since I was a teenager. But as I was saying: there we were, the three of us, watching the dancers, avoiding each other's eyes, and the mayor's husband still hadn't come back. I could exaggerate and say that I was listening to Pilar's breathing, quick and uneven like my own, but it wouldn't be true, the music was too loud, as it always is in discos. When I brought myself to look at Pilar, her face frightened me: it was as if her flesh, her features, were being absorbed by her skull, sucked into a kind of facial black hole, leaving only a trace of determination in her gaze and furrowed brow. At any rate, I realized I was in for trouble. I would swear on anything you like that Nuria had no idea what was going on. Her countenance, her beautiful perfect face, was flushed, but only because she'd just finished a string of dances, that was all. Then the tall and noble figure of Enric Gibert reemerged from the shadows. Ask her to dance, said Pilar in a peremptory tone, clearly a ploy to get them out of the way. Nuria accepted without hesitation, and I watched them from my seat, as she led the way to the dance floor, and entwined arms with the overly adroit Enric. I could feel a burning lump in my stomach. It wasn't the moment to be feeling jealous, but I was. My imagination spun out of control: I saw Nuria and the mayor's husband naked, caressing each other; I saw everybody making love, as if there had been a nuclear attack, and no one could leave the disco, and there was nothing left to restrain their passions and basic instincts; they had all become rutting animals, except for Pilar and myself, the only ones remaining cool and calm in the midst of the orgy. When I realized that Pilar was talking to me, I gave a start. I snapped out of my reverie. Where is the skating rink? she asked. I made a futile attempt to change the subject; I even mentioned her future career as a member of parliament and the way it would change her life, but it was no use; Pilar continued to inquire into the location of the skating rink, as if it made any difference. What does it matter, I said, she has to train somewhere, doesn't she? At that point Pilar spat out a pair of heavy-duty curses, and for a second I felt her lips, burning hot under the layer of lipstick, against my ear: Where is it, for fuck's sake? In the Palacio Benvingut, I thought you knew, I said. Under the table, Pilar's high heel stabbed into my groin. I must have winced because Pilar shouted a new volley of profanities into my ear. Take it easy, I whispered. Luckily the others came back at that point. They all realized; Pilar's face made it patently clear that something had spoiled her evening, but no one wanted to deal with it; on the contrary, they seemed even more bubbly than before, especially the mayor's husband, who kept joking with Nuria, while the councilors and their wives were well on their way to a grade-A bender. Just remembering those minutes makes me feel sweaty and crushed. Of course I tried to hold my head up and follow one of the conversations going on at the table (Enric, Nuria and the cultural councilor's wife were on one side, with the other wife and the two councilors opposite) but I couldn't understand a thing: it was a chaos of laughter, half-empty mixed-up glasses, and grunts and squawks unfit for human ears. Pilar, who had, apparently, been talking with the two councilors, suddenly stood up, as firm and strong as a tree, and ordered me onto the dance floor with a gesture, although I suppose she said something too. Luckily for me, they were still playing slow numbers. I say luckily because, in the first place, I was genuinely tired, and secondly because, whatever music played, Pilar was going to keep a firm hold on me so we could talk. To tell the truth, even at that moment, my admiration and affection for her remained intact. Her force of character, her obstinacy, her capacity to stand firm— those fundamental virtues of the Pilar that she was and is—could only inspire profound respect. Nevertheless, in spite of that esteem (which, I am sure, was mutual), it was the most hideous dance of my life. Wearing a skewed smile I had never seen on her face before, Pilar led me wherever she liked, and although I occasionally stumbled and seized up, in the end she had her way with me. I don't know if Nuria saw us or not, I was never brave enough to ask her; I must have been such a pitiful sight! Specifically, Pilar's interrogation focused on a single point: who else knew about the existence of the skating rink. Not when it had been built, or why, or where the money had come from, but who else was privy to the secret of its existence. I assured her that the people who had worked on the rink (who were, in fact, very few in number) had no real sense of my overall scheme. Then I told her that I was planning to present the project in detail at the council meeting in September or October, once the summer season was over. The rink could be opened to the public in December, in time for Christmas, half price for children and a big do for the inauguration. In short, I presented a wide range of uses and justifications for the facility, but nothing would calm her down. Much later, when we were all saying good night, Pilar came over to give me a kiss on the cheek, like Judas I thought, and whispered: You could ruin me, you son of a bitch. All the same, she seemed a little calmer . . .

Remo Morán:

The old lady is a colleague of yours

The old lady is a colleague of yours, said Lola that afternoon when we met in her office. That's how it began. But earlier, at midday, I had received a postcard signed by my son and sent from somewhere on the Peloponnese. It had obviously been written by Lola; for one thing, the boy hadn't yet learned to write. My ex-wife often does oddball things like that: talking as if she had Down syndrome, or like the evil child in a movie, pretending her feet are frogs and speaking for them as she wiggles her toes: Hi, I'm a frog, how are you? Actually, come to think of it, most of the women I've known could turn certain parts of their body (hands, feet, knees, navels, etc) into frogs, or elephants, or chickens that went cluck cluck and then pecked, know-it-all snakes, white crows, spiders, wayward kangaroos, when they weren't transforming their whole selves into lionesses, vampires, dolphins, eagles, mummies or hunchbacks of Notre Dame. All except Nuria, whose fingers were fingers and whose knees were always knees. Maybe we didn't have enough time, or trust each other enough, maybe our senses of humor were too different, but whatever it was, Nuria, as distinct from the others, remained herself under all circumstances, like a monolith. It's not just that she didn't turn into a mouse, sometimes it was even hard to imagine her becoming what she was generally held to be: Nuria Martí, the Olympic skater, the prettiest girl in Z. Anyway, I had received a postcard of a satyr with an erect penis, and on the other side my son had made some very funny and slightly barbed remarks about the image. It was obvious that Lola had written the card, and that she was having a good time. I was pleased that she had remembered me. About four hours later the telephone rang, and I was surprised to hear Lola's voice on the line. At first I assumed she was calling from Greece, and my first thought was that something had happened to the boy. But no, there hadn't been any kind of accident, and she wasn't phoning from Greece. They had been back for almost a week, the trip had been great, the boy got on really well with Iñaki, a pity it was only two weeks. She was calling because she needed to talk, she had a favor to ask, not really urgent, but *odd* (she stressed the word). Normally she wouldn't have asked me, but the rest of her colleagues were on holiday, she was sorry, but the only people left in the Social Services office were her and a young girl who had just started as a child welfare agent, so what could she do? The only thing she could think of was to call me. She didn't want to talk about the problem on the phone. Before hanging up I asked if she'd been too busy to call me earlier. Why? she asked. So I could see my son, I replied. He's off at camp. She sounded nervous or annoyed. At seven-thirty I walked to the Social Services office, which is in a working-class district, back from the waterfront, and a fair way from all the other government offices. The building, which is really a tiny house built in the seventies, looks run-down to say the least. After what seemed an excessive delay, Lola opened the door herself, and led me to a room at the back that looked onto a cement courtyard full of washtubs. The washtubs, which were no longer in use, held potted plants. The lights were switched off in the corridor and the rooms. There was no sign of the child welfare agent, so I presumed we were alone. In her office, Lola looked tired and happy. For a moment I thought that was how I would look too if we hadn't split up. Tired and happy. Suddenly I wanted to caress her and make love. But instead of asking if I could, I sat down and got ready to hear what she had to say to me. First we talked about the trip to Greece and about our son. Then, when we'd both had a good laugh, as we usually did, we talked about the old woman. The story went like this, as Lola told it to me: an old woman of no fixed address, who sometimes begged in the streets of Z, and called on Social Services from time to time, had come to the office the previous afternoon with a problem. She lived with a girl; the girl was sick, and the old woman didn't know what to do. The girl didn't want to go to the hospital; in fact, she didn't even know that the old woman was trying to help her. She wasn't from Z either; she'd arrived at the beginning of summer, probably from Barcelona, and didn't beg, although she sometimes kept the old woman company when she did her rounds. According to the old woman, the girl was bleeding from the mouth and nose every day. She also ate like a bird; if she went on that way she'd die for sure. The old woman thought that the girl wouldn't put up a fight if Lola went to get her and take her to the hospital. She was very emphatic about going to fetch her: if Lola or someone she could trust didn't actually go and get her, the girl would just stay in the ruins. It took me a while to understand that by "the ruins" she meant the Palacio Benvingut. That was when I began to get interested. The old woman and the girl had been living there almost since the beginning of the season. In the old woman's words, both of them were "ready for anything," the girl even had a knife, a big kitchen knife, but don't go telling. Lola didn't ask her what she meant by that, or who she was trying to keep a secret from. The old woman's a bit loopy, she explained. In the end she agreed to go, and the two of them arranged a day and a time. When it was all sorted out, the old woman (amazingly, given her age) jumped for joy a couple of times and laughed so hard Lola thought she was going to have a heart attack on the spot. As if she'd won the lottery for the blind. Soon afterward, however, Lola realized that, in her hurry, she'd forgotten that her diary was full of binding engagements, which would make it impossible for her to go to the Palacio Benvingut, but she didn't want the old woman to feel like she was being put off. Why are you so interested in her? I don't know, said Lola, she's a charming old thing, she brings me luck, I met her not long after getting pregnant. Ah, I see, I said. Incomprehensibly, my eyes filled with tears and I felt alone and lost. I'll go if you want, I said, like a man condemned to death bidding his family farewell. That's what I wanted to ask you, said Lola. It was a simple task: I had to turn up between ten and eleven the next morning at the Palacio Benvingut and drive them to the hospital. Lola would take care of the rest; she'd be free by the time we got there and she'd wait for us at the entrance. That was all. You don't think this girl with her knife is dangerous? I asked, but not seriously, more as a joke and a way to keep the conversation going. No, said Lola, it sounds like she's a physical wreck. And what was that about you or someone you trust? That's just the old lady carrying on, said Lola. I'm sure you'll find her interesting; she's a real character, and a colleague of yours, by the way. A colleague? Yes, said Lola, she used to be an artist too, in the old days . . .

GASPAR HEREDIA:

After the fat guy and the skater left

After the fat guy and the skater left, I decided to stay at
the mansion until dawn. Not inside, and certainly not in
the old storehouse where the skating rink was, but somewhere in the gardens that surrounded the building. A bit
of stealthy, watchful exploration soon revealed a suitable
place under a leafy hospitable tree, where I settled down to
wait for the first light of day. I didn't intend to fall asleep,
accustomed as I was by then to working the night shift, but
at some point, without realizing it, I must have dozed off.
When I opened my eyes, my legs were numb and the sky
was purple, with orange streaks that looked like lines traced
by skywriting planes. I was right in front of the mansion's
main door, so I decided to look for a more discreet observation post. I was vaguely hoping Caridad would come out so
I could talk to her. I remember that as I looked for a place
to continue my vigil, my heart was racing. Otherwise, I was
calm, I think. A few hours later, when the sky had turned
a faded blue, and huge dark clouds were massing on the
horizon, I saw Carmen come out of the main door. She
had the calm bearing of a housewife on her way to market;
with a bag slung over her arm and her hair combed back,
except for a sort of fringe covering part of her forehead and
her left eyebrow, she stopped on the porch, looking pleased
with herself, and glanced to the left and the right before
proceeding confidently down the steps. In the garden she

stopped again and her hawk-like gaze settled on my hiding place. With a gesture, she bid me follow her. I stepped out into the open, and together we walked slowly up the private road, as if we were enjoying a morning stroll. Carmen was not surprised to find me; on the contrary, she had been expecting me to turn up earlier. She took it for granted that I was "betrothed" to Caridad, who sooner or later, probably sooner, would return my affection, and then everyone could live "happily ever after." As we climbed the hill and gradually left the mansion behind, she compared the freshness of the morning to the sturdy good health you need to survive without love—or even with love—in hard times like these. Once again she mentioned the apartment that the council would provide for her, and, to my surprise, invited me to come and live in it. We'll need a security guard, she said with a giggle. I began to laugh. In the pines clinging to the crags I noticed some enormous-looking birds, which seemed to be laughing as well. As we came around a bend in the road and Z appeared before us, the singer's good humor suddenly vanished. To compensate, she started talking about Caridad: she didn't know much about her, but more than I did, so I listened carefully. Amid mumbled interjections, and sounding increasingly serious, she said how friendly and gentle Caridad was, how logical and clever. Then she focused on the only thing that seemed to be a real cause for concern: her lack of appetite. Caridad had simply stopped eating. As long as I'd known her, from when she was living at the campground, her diet had consisted entirely of pastries and strawberry-flavored liquid yogurt. Sometimes she'd have a coffee or a beer, mainly when she went out with Carmen to do the rounds of the cafés, but that was exceptional and, anyway, it didn't agree with her: it made her even more sullen and taciturn. On more than one occasion, Carmen had tried to get her to eat a ham sandwich, for example, but it was useless. Caridad, or her mysterious stomach, would only ingest donuts, madeleines, palm cakes, buns, spiral pastries, coconut cookies and other sweet things. What did she have for breakfast? Nothing, not even a gulp of water. And for lunch? Caridad got up at one or two in the afternoon, so she didn't have lunch either. An afternoon snack? For a snack she would have a donut and a madeleine, which she took from a box secreted in one of the mansion's rooms, where the two of them kept their provisions, safe from rats and ants. Nothing else? Perhaps a thimbleful of liquid yogurt before dinner. And dinner? Dinner, which they usually ate together, consisted of two or three donuts and a few mouthfuls of liquid yogurt. Caridad was really crazy about donuts. And liquid yogurt. Naturally, she had lost weight, and now you could even count her ribs, but Caridad's willpower and her bird-like diet were indissolubly wedded. However she looked at it, Carmen couldn't understand how Caridad had survived so long on such piffling nourishment, but she had, she was surviving, and she was even "prettier every day." When we reached the streets of Z, I offered to buy her lunch. Carmen ordered *churros* and hot chocolate. The waiter, a sleepy teenager who was in no mood for kidding, said they didn't have any, so she made do with a beer and a ladyfinger. Talking too much made her thirsty. I ordered a coffee with milk and two donuts. Before we said good-bye, she asked me if I had ever been inside the mansion. I said no. Wise choice, she said, but she didn't believe me . . .

Enric Rosquelles:

The day after the party at the disco

The day after the party at the disco that wretched old woman came bursting into my office. The morning was calm, as if wrapped in a quiet, damp towel, although the calm was only apparent, or rather confined to one side of the morning, the left side, say, while chaos was seething on the right-hand side, a chaos that only I could hear and sense. To be quite honest, I should say that from the moment I opened my eyes, I began to feel anxious, as if I could smell disaster even in the air of my bedroom. As I drove to Z, after a shower and breakfast, that feeling, which was not entirely new to me, diminished in intensity, but the irrational aspects of the problem remained, there in the car and later in the office, if you see what I mean; they remained with me in attenuated form, as a sense of foreboding. I felt I could actually see things and people aging second by second, all of them swept along in a time-stream flowing inexorably toward misery and grief. Then the door of the office swung open with a dull thud, and the old woman appeared, followed by my secretary, who, half aggrieved, half annoyed, was trying to shepherd her back into the waiting room. The old lady was thin and her hair was unevenly cut; she fixed her little eyes on me, in a brief intense examination, before announcing that she had something to tell me. At first I didn't even stand up; I was absorbed in my own premonitions, and incidents like this are not unusual, given the nature of my work. A high proportion of our clients suppose that by going to management they will finally get their problems solved. In such cases, armed with kind words and a great deal of patience, I direct them to the offices located in the district of M, where they will be helped by our social workers and child welfare agents. I was on the point of doing just that when the old woman, after checking that it was me and not someone else observing her calmly from the other side of the desk, winked at me and softly uttered her talismanic sentence: I was hoping to discuss the business of the skating rink, either with you or with the mayor. Everything I had been suspecting and fearing since I woke up that morning materialized at once, taking shape with devastating force, as if I had stepped into a science-fiction movie. It would not be an exaggeration to say that I nearly collapsed into a mass of trembling jelly. Nevertheless, I steeled myself and managed to prevent my nerves from giving me away. Feigning a sudden and cheerful interest, I asked my secretary to leave us alone. She released the old woman, whom she had been holding by the arm, and looked at me as if she couldn't believe what she was hearing. I had to repeat the order; then she left my office and shut the door behind her. The infamous discussion that is supposed to have taken place between the old woman and myself is, of course, a fabrication, one of many. From my secretary's desk you can't hear anything that is said in my office, unless it is shouted, and I can assure you that there were no shouts, or threats, or screams. The door remained shut throughout. My spirits, as you can well imagine, were about as low as they could be. The adjective "exhausted" gives a fair description of my state of mind, faced with that old woman; she, however, seemed to be possessed of boundless energy and vitality. As she spoke, sometimes in a normal tone of voice, sometimes in whispers, the way she gestured with her hands was consistently reminiscent of a movie about pharaohs and pyramids. From that torrent of nonsense, I gathered that she wanted a subsidized apartment, a "pension or financial aid," and a job for some unnamed monster. None of those things, I said, were within my power. Then she demanded to see the mayor. Somehow she associated both of us with the existence of the skating rink. I asked her what she hoped to get out of a meeting with the mayor, and her reply confirmed my fears: Pilar, the old woman felt, would be more sympathetic to her requests. I said it wasn't necessary, I'd see what I could do to sort out her situation, and immediately pulled out my wallet and gave her ten thousand pesetas, which the old woman put straight into her pocket. Then, trying to sound relaxed, I explained that for the moment I couldn't do anything about the subsidized apartment, but when the season was over, say mid-September, I'd look into it, and try to find her something. The old woman inquired about her pension. I pulled out a sheet of paper and took down some details: there again, I explained, the problem was that until the rest of the municipal staff came back from vacation, nothing could be done. The old woman looked thoughtful for a while, but soon it was clear that, for the time being at least, the matter was in abeyance. Before taking her leave, she said that this deal would wipe the slate clean, and she was prepared to put our previous differences behind her. Unable to conceal my surprise, I assured her that we could hardly have had previous differences since this was the first time we had met. Then the old woman cast her mind back; it turned out that, some years before, she had paid a visit to Social Services. She recalled the past in clear and precise words that set me trembling from head to foot. You have to understand, I was sitting behind my desk and that damn witch, speaking those oily-smooth, razor-sharp words, was painting a picture in which only she and I existed, and neither had any chance of escape. But now the slate is clean, she said, with a sparkle in her eyes. I nodded. I knew I hadn't fooled her with any of my lies. I felt the way any of you would have felt: trapped . . .

Remo Morán:

At exactly ten in the morning I got into my car and set off

At exactly ten in the morning I got into my car and set off
for the Palacio Benvingut. It was a foggy day and the bends
on the highway to Y are notoriously hazardous, so I drove
with extreme care. There wasn't much traffic and I had no
trouble finding the palace, which had always intrigued me,
because of the legend of its creator and first owner, but also
because of its bewildering architecture. Like so many unin-
habited houses on the Costa Brava and in the Maresme,
the mansion had conserved its beauty even in ruins. The
garden's iron gates were open, but not far enough to let a
car through. I got out and opened them right up. The
hinges made an awful screeching noise. For a moment I
considered continuing on foot, but then I thought better
of it and returned to the car. There was a considerable distance from the main gate to the house itself, and the road,
half gravel, half dirt, was lined with anemic shrubs and der-
elict flower beds. In the garden, a few enormous trees reared
skyward, and beyond them, bushes grew wild among pavil-
ions and ruined fountains, forming a dense, black-green
wall. On the façade of the mansion, I discovered an inscription. It's the sort of thing that only happens by seren-
dipity; if someone had told me to look for the inscription,
I'd never have been able to find it. With letters chiseled into
the stone, the house said, in Catalan: "Benvingut made
me." The blue of the façade, shaded from the sun, seemed

to confirm the assertion: I am as I am because Benvingut made me so. I left the car parked by the porch and knocked on the door. No one answered. I thought the house must be empty; even my own presence, as I stood there waiting, seemed no more imposing than the weeds growing all around. After a moment of hesitation I decided to go and take a look around the back. A stone path ran along under the shuttered windows of the first floor to an archway, beyond which lay another garden, at a lower level than the one I had just crossed, surrounded by walls and terraces, on each of which I noticed the mutilated remains of a statue. Each of the steps leading up to the terraces was decorated with a little cornucopia carved in the stone, almost at ground level. At the far end, a wooden lattice door opened onto a patio which directly overlooked the sea. Part of the house was built on the rocks, or rather hollowed out of the rocky promontory, clasping it in a cryptic embrace, and to one side, next to the stairways that went winding down to the beach, stood an enormous wooden structure, with protruding beams, a cross between a barn and a Protestant church, blighted by time and neglect, but still sound. The large sheet-metal doors were open. I went in. Inside, someone animated by a fierce childish willfulness had used an enormous number of packing cases to build a series of awkward passages, with walls about nine feet high for a start, but dropping to just over a foot and a half as you went further in. The passages formed concentric circles around the skating rink. In the center of the rink was a dark huddled mass, black like some of the beams running clear across the ceiling. Blood, from various parts of the fallen body, had flowed in all directions, forming patterns and geometrical figures that I mistook at first for shadows. In some places it had almost reached the edge of the rink. Kneeling down, feeling dizzy and nauseated, I observed how the ice had begun to absorb and harden around all that butchery. In a corner of the rink I spotted the knife. I didn't go over to take a closer look, much less touch it; from where I was, I could see clearly that it was a kitchen knife, with a broad blade and a plastic handle. The bloodstains on the handle were visible even at a distance. After a while I approached the body gingerly, trying not to slip on the ice or step in the congealed puddles of blood. I had known straight away that she was dead, but from close up she seemed to be sleeping, and the one eye I could see without shifting her had a slightly disgruntled look. Presuming that she was the old woman who had gone to see Lola, I squatted there for a long time, staring at her as if under hypnosis, irrationally expecting Nuria to appear at the scene of the crime. The skating rink seemed to have some kind of magnetic pull, although, from what I could see, all its potential users and visitors had vanished a good while ago, and I was the last to appear. When I stood up, my legs were frozen. Outside, clouds had entirely filled the sky and a threatening wind was beginning to blow from the sea. I know I should have retraced my steps, gone back to Z and informed the police, but I didn't. Instead, I took several deep breaths and tried to get the blood flowing in my legs—they weren't just cold, I was starting to get cramps—and then, as if something in there was attracting me irresistibly, I went back into the storehouse, and wandered around the circular passages, looking absently at the packing cases, counting the spotlights aimed at the rink, trying to imagine what had happened in that glacial enclave. Taking care not to leave any fingerprints, I climbed on top of some cases and surveyed the storehouse. From that vantage point I had a panoramic view of what looked like a labyrinth with a frozen center, marked by a black hole: the body. I could also see that in one of the other walls, half hidden by the cases, there was another door. I went straight to it. And after climbing a staircase and walking down a gallery that opened onto the terraced garden, I found myself wandering through the endless corridors of the Palacio Benvingut. I soon lost count of the rooms I had passed through or looked into. Predictably, most of them were in a state of utter neglect: thick dust, cobwebs, paint flaking off the walls. In some rooms the wind had forced the windows, and the walls and floor bore witness to the rains of the last thirty years. In others, the windows had been firmly nailed to the frames, and the smell of rot was unbearable. Surprisingly, on the first floor I found two rooms that had been recently painted, with some carpenter's tools lying outside in the hallway. I still don't know exactly what drove me to search the whole house. In a kind of reading room shaped like a horseshoe, on the top floor, under a window looking out over the sea, I found Gasparín wrapped up in ragged tartan rugs, with a girl apparently asleep beside him. Days later he confessed to me that when he heard my steps he thought it was the police, and there was nowhere to run. Behind them, on the wall, above the single, magnificent window, was the following inscription: CORAJE, CANEJO ("*Courage, damn it*"). The letters, which had faded over the years, were all capitals, and weirdly shaped, like the rest of the house, which left me in no doubt as to who had written them. Benvingut, the Indian. But that was odd, because as far as I knew, Benvingut had lived, traveled and made his fortune in Cuba, Mexico and the United States, while the expression was Argentinean or Uruguayan. And it was stranger still to have painted it in a reading room, where a maxim in Latin or Greek would be more appropriate, especially since it stared you in the face as soon as you opened the door. That is, if the room had ever served its ostensible function, which I was beginning to doubt. In any case, I wasn't surprised that Gasparín had chosen to wait in that place for what he supposed was imminent. We didn't say a word, just looked at each other, me in the doorway and him on the floor, under the inscription, with his arm around the sleeping girl. It was a pity to speak and wake her from what seemed such a calm and happy sleep. What do I remember most clearly about that moment? Gasparín's eyes and the blood-stained cheeks of the girl. When I finally broke the silence, and asked if he knew what was downstairs, on the rink, he nodded. For a moment I imagined him stabbing the old woman, but I knew straight away in my heart that he couldn't have. Then I told him to get up and go. I can't leave her, he said. Take her with you. Where? asked Gasparín with a touch of sarcasm. The campground, I said, wait for me there. Gasparín nodded. The girl was moving but she seemed to be still asleep. Try to keep a low profile, I said as they left the palace. I went back to the ice rink and wiped the prints from the knife with my handkerchief; then I got in the car and drove back to Z. I had put the old tartan rugs that Gasparín and the girl had been using in the trunk. I saw them before I reached the town: they were walking along the highway, with their arms around each other, in something of a hurry, as if they were worried about the approaching rain. I had never seen Gasparín with his arm around a girl, although I had known him since he was nineteen and I was twenty. The highway seemed very broad and the sea much broader still, and they were like two blind stubborn dwarves. I don't think they recognized the car; in fact I think they hardly noticed it. On my way to the hospital, I got stuck in heavy traffic. When I finally got there,

Lola was gone. I found her in her office, where I told her everything, except for my encounter with Gasparín and the sleeping girl. For a while we discussed what to do. Lola seemed distraught. I should never have asked you to help me out, she said. Do you think the girl with the knife killed her? I don't think any such girl exists, I said. Then we rang the police . . .

GASPAR HEREDIA:

Until El Carajillo fell asleep we talked about women

Until El Carajillo fell asleep we talked about women, food, work, children, illness and death . . . When I heard him snoring, I switched off the light in the office and went outside to pursue my reflections. At dawn I went back into the office, told El Carajillo there was nothing to report, and said I had to get going. Still half asleep, El Carajillo mumbled some incomprehensible words. Something about a gigantic tear. A titanic tear. I thought he must have been dreaming about the lyrics of a song. Then he opened one eye and asked me where I was going. Just out for a walk, I said. He wished me luck and went back to sleep. Walking briskly, I estimated, it would take me forty-five minutes to reach the Palacio Benvingut. I had plenty of time, so before leaving town, I stopped for breakfast in a cantina full of fishermen. I didn't pay much attention to what they were saying, but I think it was something about a whale that had been spotted by several boats and a fisherman who had been lost at sea. At the back of the bar, surrounded by men in oilskins, a kid who must have been about fourteen was gesturing wildly, laughing, then groaning, repeating words that others had spoken that night. "The Accident," "The Whale," "The Big Man," "The Wave" rang out like winning lottery numbers. I paid and left inconspicuously. On my way out to the mansion, I didn't see a single car heading for Z or Y, or anyone walking in either direction. Viewed from the top of the coves, the town seemed to be asleep; no doubt only the fishermen were awake. A few boats were still working near the beach. When I finally reached the mansion, I automatically went straight to the skating rink. The lights were on, so I thought the skater and the fat guy might be there. But no, inside, I saw poor Carmen, and in the fat guy's usual place, at the edge of the rink, Caridad, staring at the body. Her eyes were blurry, the way they used to be in the campground at night. Her face was covered with blood; it was running from her nose. She didn't realize I was there until I put my hands on her shoulders. For some reason I felt that if she stepped onto the ice, which I thought she was about to do, I would lose her forever. There was blood on her T-shirt and her hands. Both of us were shaking. As I held her shoulders, my arms were as limp as cables and my chattering teeth made a sound in keeping with the scene. Caridad was trembling too, but the movement was coming from deep inside and returning to its source, in a secret circuit perceptible only to the sense of touch. I even thought that my trembling was induced by hers, and would stop if I let go of her, but I didn't. It was only when she felt my hands on her shoulders that Caridad looked at me, as if I was a stranger, as if she believed that I had killed the singer. What happened, I asked? She didn't reply. The knife, the ice, the morning, the singer's body, the mansion, Caridad's eyes, everything began to spin . . . I gripped her shoulders as if I was afraid that she was going to disappear. I remembered how kind and generous the singer had been with Caridad, and how kind and generous Caridad had been with the singer. Outsiders in Z, they had helped each other as best they could throughout that summer. It took a few moments to turn my gaze away from the body lying on the ice. Then I said we should leave, although I suspected we had no place to go. I pushed Caridad gently toward the mansion. She let herself be guided with a docility that surprised me. Let's go and get your things, I said. Before we knew it, we were roaming through the building, along corridors, up and down stairs, more and more hurriedly, as if our ultimate departure from the scene of the crime was conditional on searching the building from top to bottom. I remember whispering in her ear at some point as we wandered on that I was the night watchman from the campground, that she could trust me, but I don't think she heard. The room that Caridad and Carmen had been sleeping in was on the second floor. It was no bigger than a pantry and you had to go through two other rooms to reach it, so it was fairly inconspicuous and hard to find. Change your T-shirt, I said. Caridad took a black T-shirt from her backpack and threw the bloody one on the floor. I crouched down, picked up all her things, including the bloody T-shirt, and put them in the pack. The rest of the stuff belonged to the singer: empty bottles, candles, plastic bags full of clothes, comics, plates, glasses. There's no hurry, said Caridad. I looked at her in the semidarkness: one night in that room the two women had heard the chords of the "Fire Dance," and it must had given them a fright. I imagined them going down the stairs toward the music, all on their own in the dark world, one with the knife, the other with a stick or a bottle, toward the dazzling brilliance of the skating rink. Or maybe not, in any case it didn't matter now. When we left the room, Caridad took the lead. Instead of going downstairs we went up to a room on the third floor. Stay with me until they come, said Caridad, looking me in the eye. I assumed she was referring to the police. We'll go down for this together, I thought. Both of us were chilled to the bone, so we wrapped ourselves in the blankets and curled up on the wooden floor. Dim rays of light were filtering in through the window. It was like camping. Probably because of the shared warmth, I was asleep before I knew it. The sound of steps downstairs woke me. Someone was opening and shutting doors. It's illogical and silly, I know, but instead of assuming it was the police, my first thought was: It's Carmen, risen from her puddle of blood and come to look for us. Not to seek vengeance or scare us, but to settle down beside us, snug among the blankets. Of course I had absolutely no idea what time it was. When the door opened to reveal Remo Morán, I wasn't all that surprised. I remembered the night I saw him coming out of the disco with a blonde girl, the skater, so it didn't seem strange that he should come looking for her. You're my father, I thought. Help me. I think Remo was afraid that Caridad might be dead too . . .

Enric Rosquelles:

In the afternoon Pilar called my office to inform me

In the afternoon Pilar called my office to inform me, in a dry and official tone, that a body had been discovered at the Palacio Benvingut. The receiver fell out of my hand, and when I picked it up, there was no one at the other end. As I was dialing Nuria's number I realized I was shaking, but I pulled myself together, and when Laia answered the phone I was able to ask for her sister in a reasonably steady voice. Nuria wasn't there. Under normal circumstances I would never have dared to ask if she had come home the previous night, but circumstances were not normal. Laia giggled teasingly before answering. Yes, what did I think? Of course she had come home last night. I sighed with relief and asked her to get Nuria to contact me as soon as possible. If she didn't call me within the next half hour, I would be coming around to the apartment. You're jealous, said Laia. No, I said, I'm not jealous. She started asking what was going on, poor kid, but I was at my wits' end, I had to hang up. I desperately needed to think, so I took some deep breaths and tried to give myself another dose of calm. I had almost succeeded when there was a knock at the door: it was old García, the municipal police chief. He was holding a bundle of papers and wearing his usual good-natured expression, although it was looking a little strained. He asked if he could sit down for a while. Don't stand in the doorway, come in, take a seat, make yourself at home, I said. I think I raised my voice a bit. Shrugging his shoulders, he walked over to the chair I had offered him, and for a moment we both remained silent: he sat with his knees wide apart, while I stood looking out of the window at the street. Come on, spit it out, I said, cutting to the chase. García advised me to lower my voice. The secretary can hear you, he said, but he said it so quietly I had to ask him to repeat himself. Feeling despondent but slightly calmer, I sat down and decided to try the unblinking stare. As I had anticipated, García averted his gaze almost immediately, looking instead at the diplomas hanging on the wall. You have lots of qualifications, he observed in a whisper. I nodded without taking my eyes off him. Yes, those were my trophies, proof of my intelligence and dedication: the photocopy of my psychology degree (my mother has the framed original), and diplomas from the numerous short courses I have done, on special education, youth work, teaching in prison, first aid and community medical centers and drop-in centers, juvenile delinquency and drug addiction, socio-cultural event organization, urban psychology, criminal psychology (two days, in Paris), social education (a weekend in Cologne, with vaguely Nazi instructors), psychosocial motivation, psychology and the environment, aging and the aged, rehabilitation centers and camps, *Toward a Socialist Europe*, Spanish politics and economics, politics and sports in Spain, politics and the Third World, problems and solutions in small municipalities, etc, etc. I didn't know you'd studied so much, said García with a sigh. I declined to reply; my mind, as the saying goes, was miles away, lost in a fantasy land. Without realizing, I'd started to hum the "Fire Dance." García cleared his throat and said, You know why I'm here. I don't like being interrupted, who does? It seemed grossly impolite, but what else could I expect from a policeman? Get to the point, get to the point, I said, raising my voice again. García blushed so deeply I thought he was going to have a heart attack or a stroke or both at once. You're under arrest, he said, looking at the floor. There you go, see: it wasn't that hard, I said with a smile, and God knows what an effort it took to keep that smile on my face. Then, when the smile had eventually faded, I asked what I was supposed to have done. Murdered a woman, said García, and embezzlement. Although I had a slight hunch, I was genuinely curious to know whom I was supposed to have killed, so I asked. A beggar, said García, looking through his papers: Carmen González Medrano. I asked if he had reached that conclusion on his own, or if it was a collective effort. García shrugged his shoulders as if he didn't understand. If you think you're going to score points at my expense, you've got another think coming, I warned him. García replied that it wasn't about scoring anything, and he really regretted having to arrest me, but I had to understand, he was only doing his job. I didn't believe a word he said, you could see the joy sparkling in his eyes: for the first time in his life, the son of a bitch had got in ahead of the national police and the *guardia civil*. If you think you're going to get your picture in the paper, you better watch out, García, I bellowed, because there's a big surprise in store for you and the others. García was mumbling something in reply when the phone rang and I lunged forward, as if my life depended on it. Nuria's voice at the other end of the line was like a bird shivering in the cold. I swear I had never felt so close to her. Nuria, I said, Nuria, Nuria, Nuria. To give him his due, García was discreet; he stood up, turned his back on me and looked at the diplomas. Before I knew it, I began to cry. Somehow Nuria realized and, sounding unsure and very worried, she asked if I was crying, a conjecture that I hastened to correct in word and deed. García was glancing at me sideways from a corner. I could hear shouting outside: it was my secretary, and other voices that I couldn't recognize, making requests and demands. Quite a racket, in any case. Right then, I would gladly have volunteered to be smitten by a thunderbolt. United by the telephone line, Nuria's breathing and mine mingled in a timeless marriage: the bond, the consummation and the passing of our quiet days—our secret. My teeth started grinding horribly. What's happening? asked Nuria. I noticed that García had approached me again and was grimacing incomprehensibly. The noises from outside were getting louder: chairs falling over, bodies bumping against the walls, someone shouting, Be quiet and calm down, please, we don't want to have to charge you with obstruction of justice. Then I uttered, syllable by syllable: Nu-ri-a-I-have-to-hang-up-what-ev-er-hap-pens-re-mem-ber-I-love-you-re-mem-ber-I-love-you . . .

Remo Morán:

The policemen were young and they didn't look too smart

The policemen were young and they didn't look too smart, although on the way there one of them said he had a degree in economics. The other one was an amateur mechanic, crazy about motorbikes; whenever he could get away, he went racing at the various meets in Catalonia and Valencia. Both were married and had kids. They weren't so chatty when they got to Lola's office, although after listening to my story and scribbling a bit in a none-too-clean notebook, they looked at each other as if thinking, This could be our big day. They decided to set off immediately for the Palacio Benvingut. A little apprehensively, they asked me to accompany them. Lola didn't want me to go on my own (I don't know what she thought might happen) and insisted on joining the group; after all, she was the only one who would be able to identify the body. When Lola had located the victim's record card in a bulging file, the four of us left for the crime scene in the patrol car, an arrangement that I was to regret later on, because it meant I had to go back to Lola's office to get my car, and by then I didn't have much time or energy to spare. Nothing had changed at the Palacio Benvingut, except that the general impression of desolation, the atmosphere of premature autumn enveloping the house and its surroundings, had perhaps intensified. The body was still there, but the spilt blood didn't seem as sinister, nor as red. Lola took a couple of steps on the ice and identified the victim without difficulty: Carmen González Medrano, vagrant. Later on, the police chief turned up to congratulate his officers, along with a kind of coroner, followed by three guys from the Red Cross and then a young woman of about thirty who identified herself as the local judge. She and Lola knew each other. They wrangled over the beggar's record card. The judge wanted to keep it, but Lola flatly refused. Watching the two of them argue, both so young and energetic, I thought, This is the new Spain, striding boldly toward the future. By contrast, the old woman and I, nostalgic or passive or maybe just patient, were like two arrows flying back into the past, one quickly, the other in very slow motion. Finally, thanks to the coroner's mediation, the women reached an agreement: Lola would keep the card and send a photocopy to the judge. As for me, I had to repeat my story a couple of times, and when we were allowed to go there was no one left to give us a lift. We walked back to Z. Lola looked slightly pale but very pretty. At first she told me what little she knew about the dead woman, but we ended up talking about her recent trip to Greece and what our son had got up to. In the afternoon, after various fruitless attempts to get in touch with Nuria, I decided to go to her apartment again and find out where she was. Her mother opened the door but didn't invite me in. Her eyes were red and she was clearly in no mood for conversation. Nuria had gone to Barcelona. She didn't know when she'd be back. At the hotel, Alex was waiting for me with a bombshell: the police had arrested Enric Rosquelles on suspicion of murder. I was obliged to repeat the story I had already told hundreds of times that morning; then I went up to my room to think. But instead I fell asleep, sitting on the sofa, and dreamed that bird-women, gathering in a flock outside, near the balcony, were looking at me through the windows, their wings beating quietly in the warm humid air. One by one I began to recognize them: Lola and Nuria, and other women from Z, although their faces were blurry so I couldn't be sure. The old woman was fluttering in the middle, like a queen surrounded by her entourage. She was the only one really watching me. A gust blew the windows open and I felt her voice, just as the group of bird-women began to rise and clouds came down over the town. Even so, the dead woman's voice made the windowpanes shake. She was singing. The words of her song were simple and repetitive: Avenge me, avenge me, avenge me—dear colleague, avenge me, avenge me, avenge me. Just before I woke up, I heard myself promising that I would, but first I had to find her killer. That night, after taking a shower, I went out for a walk and headed for Stella Maris. Gasparín, El Carajillo and a camper in a T-shirt were sitting outside the office, enjoying the cool of the evening. I stopped to chat for a while. Then I told Gasparín and El Carajillo to follow me. When we were alone on a path in the campground, I asked Gasparín where the girl was. Sleeping, he said, in my tent. Do you know where we found her? I asked El Carajillo. I can guess, he said. Well forget it, or keep it quiet until things are sorted out. That's fine by me, said El Carajillo, but there might be a problem when the police get hold of her. They won't, I said, and if they do, she'll leave us out of it. We can trust her, can't we? Gasparín didn't reply. I repeated the question. It depends, said Gasparín, some people can, others can't. Can I, for example? Yes, said Gasparín, I think so. El Carajillo too. And what about you? I don't know, said Gasparín, what I'm trying to work out is whether she can trust me. We agreed that it would be best if both he and the girl kept a low profile. The police could find you through her, though the way things are going I don't think they will. Gasparín was an illegal immigrant in Spain and as for his girlfriend, God only knew. When we went back to reception, the guy in the T-shirt was still there, and he started asking all sorts of questions about what had happened at the Palacio Benvingut. He told me it had been on the TV3 news, and it sounded like the scandal was just beginning . . .

GASPAR HEREDIA:

Caridad adapted pretty well to life at the campground

Caridad adapted pretty well to life at the campground, although it was hard to tell at the start, because she rarely spoke, and I rarely asked her a question. Rather than really sharing the tent, we took turns in it: when I was getting ready for bed, she was waking up, and by the time I got up, she had already gone to sleep. We only had one meal together, the morning meal—dinner for me, breakfast for her—consisting of cheese, yogurt, fruit, boiled ham, and whole wheat bread, a diet designed to put some color back into her cheeks, although she remained reluctant to eat. If by chance we happened to be in the campground bar at the same time, we'd usually have a beer together. We didn't talk much, but I soon discovered that she had the most disturbing voice I have ever heard. It was intensely pleasurable to crawl into the tent and find her smell clinging to the mess of clothes. It was even better to wake up and find her a few steps away from the tent, sitting on the ground, reading by the light of a gas lamp. The singer had told me about her ill health, but the only sign of it I could see was frequent bleeding from the nose, which according to Caridad was caused by the sun, no big deal. The worst thing was that sometimes she didn't notice until the blood started dripping from her chin, and, if you didn't know about her condition, it was a disquieting sight. When she got a nosebleed, every two days or so, she'd hold a damp handkerchief against her nasal septum, and lie on the ground face up beside the tent, waiting for it to stop. I exploited those opportunities to talk with her as tactfully as I could. I would start with the weather and end with her health. Naturally, whenever I suggested we go see a doctor, she flatly refused. Caridad, as I later found out, hated hospitals as much as she hated schools, police stations and old people's homes. I never saw her bleed from the mouth or spit blood, which led me to suspect that Carmen had been mistaken or maybe, encouraged by my obvious interest, had exaggerated her friend's ills. I never found out whether Caridad had parents, brothers, sisters or any other relatives. She kept her past sealed in the strictest silence, which was surprising for someone who hadn't even reached the age of twenty. One day she ran into the boy with the motorbike in the campground bar. I saw them before I got there, and rather than going up to them or walking away, I watched from a distance. They spoke—the boy did, anyway, while Caridad moved her lips from time to time—for about ten minutes. Two charged-up batteries, I thought. Then they went their separate ways, like spaceships on diverging trajectories, and the vibrant emptiness they left in the bar threatened to swallow up the other clients. Another day, while we were having a beer, the boy appeared and started talking. He was speaking Spanish but using words that it seemed only he and Caridad could understand. Before leaving he smiled at me in a way that could have meant anything. The next time I saw him was at reception; he rode up on his bike, and said he wanted to talk to me. It turned out he only wanted to thank me for what I had done for Caridad. She's out of her tree, he said, but she's a good person. It was nighttime and the motorbike was making quite a racket. I told him to switch off the motor and push it to his tent, which he did.

For many days, Caridad and I didn't leave the campground except to buy provisions. We didn't plan it that way; it was just that for different reasons neither of us felt like going out. I could have gone on like that forever, but the boy with the motorbike took to visiting every afternoon, coming straight to our tent without any kind of pretext. Still half asleep, I'd hear him arrive and start up a conversation with Caridad, who by that time, unless she'd gone to the bar, would be sitting outside the tent, with a book, but not reading, just thinking. One afternoon the boy came with his motorbike, and after talking in hushed voices for a couple of minutes, the pair of them disappeared. I thought I wouldn't see her again. When they came back, at three or four in the morning, I was sitting beside the entrance barrier, and Caridad greeted me with a nod. Two days later the boy left the campground and Caridad stayed with me. At the time, El Carajillo told me, the town was in turmoil, on edge. The embezzlement was bigger news than the crime at the Palacio Benvingut, but I had no idea what was going on: I wasn't buying newspapers or listening to the radio, and I only watched TV now and then in the office. Remo came to see me a few times. We did our best to make small talk, but it was pretty hopeless. A sorry performance. We couldn't even look each other in the eye. It was only when he started going on and on about the old days in Mexico (I just listened) that it got a bit more animated. Animated but sad. Just as well we didn't sink to reading our new poems. Though maybe that was because we didn't have any. One night I saw the fat guy on TV: he was being escorted by two policemen from a car to a courtroom. He didn't try to cover his face with his jacket or his cuffed hands; on the contrary, he looked at the camera with a curious, distant gaze, as if the whole business had nothing to do with him, as if the killers and embezzlers were on the other side, well out of the camera's range. One night, while I was sleeping, Caridad came into the tent, got undressed, and we made love, a bit like the guy on TV, as if it had nothing to do with us, as if the real lovers were dead and buried. But it was the first time and it was beautiful, and from then on we began to talk a bit more, not a lot, but a bit more . . .

Enric Rosquelles:

I swear I didn't kill her

I swear I didn't kill her. I'd only seen her a couple of times in my life; why would I want to kill her? It's true that the old woman came to my office and I gave her money, yes, you could even say she was blackmailing me, but that's no reason to kill anyone. I'm a Catalan and this is Catalonia, not Chicago or Colombia. And with a *knife* as well! I have never attacked anyone with a knife, not even in my dreams, and supposing, just supposing, that I had—can you seriously imagine me stabbing her twenty times? Sorry, thirty-four times, to be exact. Come on! And right in the middle of my skating rink! I might as well have killed myself straight away if I'd done that, because I was always going to be the prime suspect for a murder committed in the Palacio Benvingut. And what could I possibly have to gain by killing the old woman? Nothing, only grief, as if I didn't have enough of that already. Since the day that wretched woman died my life has been a nightmare. Everyone has turned their back on me. They fired me and kicked me out of the party. No one wanted to hear my version of the story. After all the help I gave her, Pilar is saying she'd had doubts about me for some time. A barefaced lie. And the party secretary in Gerona is saying he'd always thought there was something suspicious about me. Another lie. Stupid lies, too! If it was so obvious what I was up to, and they knew, why didn't they do something before embezzlement and murder were committed? I'm telling you: the reason they didn't do anything is that they didn't know or suspect what was going on; they had no idea. The best thing for them to do now would be keep their mouths shut and face up to their individual responsibilities. Yes, I used public funds to build the skating rink at the Palacio Benvingut, but I have documentation here to prove that the rink can pay for itself within seven years, if it's well run, not to mention the benefits to the local athletic community and skaters from further afield, since there is no adequate facility for winter sports anywhere in the region. And let me point out, to those who think I'm making up excuses and justifications after the fact, that's a proper, regulation-size rink, 184 by 85 feet, the minimum size (the maximum is 197 by 98). All we'd have to do is add a "decent and appropriate" dressing room (as the regulations specify) and simple but comfortable seating, and practically overnight Z would have a real treasure for years to come, the envy of all the neighboring towns, every bit as good as any competition rink in Europe. All right, so no one authorized me to spend public funds on a sports facility. So I did it behind everyone's back, especially behind the backs of the communists and Convergencia i Unión. So my motivation was personal, I wanted to win the favors of a skater. Does that mean I'm a madman, a megalomaniac, and probably, though we're still waiting for proof, a killer? I'm sorry to disappoint you, but it isn't true, I'm not a monster, just an enterprising, tenacious administrator, and I acted in good faith. For example, the plans for the rink didn't cost a cent; I created them myself, drawing on the work of the famous engineer Harold Petersson, the designer of Rome's first skating rink, built at the behest of Benito Mussolini in 1932. The refrigerator grille is my own invention, although it was inspired by the energy-efficient grilles used by the functionalist architects John F. Mitchell and James Brandon, who specialized in sports facilities. I didn't have to excavate: I filled in Benvingut's old swimming pool. I was able to buy most of the machinery at bargain prices from a friend in Barcelona, an entrepreneur bankrupted by the influx of foreign firms. To secure the services and the discretion of Z's most notorious builder, all I had to do was apply a little pressure (and he in turn applied pressure to his laborers). No one will admit it now, but the operation was tightly run. I ask you: who else could have managed a project like that, keeping it quiet and spending so little money? People are throwing around figures of 20, 30 or even 40 million pesetas, but I can assure you that the sum I appropriated was a fraction of that. Anyway, I know that no one can honestly stand up and say: I could have done it better. Not that I'm trying to present myself as some kind of moral example. I know I did something I shouldn't have done. I know I made a mistake. Pilar will probably lose the election because of me. I have brought the party into disrepute. Without meaning to, I set loose the pack of wolves that is after Nuria. I was the laughingstock of Spain for at least two nights, and the laughingstock of Catalonia for a whole week. The most contemptible sport shows on the airwaves have dragged my name through the mud. But to go on and call me a murderer is an enormous jump. I swear I didn't kill her; the night of the murder I was at home, sleeping fitfully, tangled in nightmares and sheets damp with sweat. Unfortunately my poor mother is a sound sleeper, so she cannot vouch for me . . .

REMO MORÁN:

The newspapers and magazines made her famous

The newspapers and magazines made her famous throughout the country, and they say the story even went international; her photo appeared in sensationalist weeklies across Europe. They called her The Mystery Woman of the Palacio Benvingut, The Ice Maiden, The Angel-Eyed Skater, The Spanish Object of Desire, The Beauty who Rocked the Costa Brava. Not long after the news broke, she was expelled from the Federation, which killed any hopes she might have had of returning to competition skating. A Barcelona magazine offered her two million pesetas for a naked photo shoot. Another one offered her half a million for the complete story of what had happened at the Palacio Benvingut. Some said that Enric Rosquelles was taking the rap for Nuria, but that accusation didn't stand up: according to the pathologists, the crime took place around three in the morning, and Nuria was at home that night; her mother and sister confirmed it. If that wasn't enough to make her alibi watertight, a friend of hers from X had spent the night at the apartment, for reasons irrelevant to the case, and they had talked until after the estimated time of death and slept in the same room. The friend stated unequivocally that Nuria stayed in bed for the rest of the night. The hardest thing of all for her was being debarred from the skating team; she wasn't even allowed to compete in the selection trials. Suddenly, just when everything seemed to be going so well, the scholarships and the medals came to an end, along with the hopes of more to come. While the story was still fresh, and the media were still keen to interview her, especially the scandal-mongering late-night sport shows, she took every opportunity to speak out against the managers and trainers who had set themselves up as judges and arbitrarily shut her out of what was, to her, far more than a profession. She claimed it was unconstitutional and tried to defend herself, but it was futile. One night when I was in the bar with Alex and a waiter, after all the clients had gone, I heard her on the radio. That little transistor radio was like a ghost from another planet, between a box of beers and the fridge. I shouldn't have listened, it was excruciating: the host manipulated her for twenty minutes, expertly violating her privacy, cloaking his rapacity in concern. Nuria came back to Z a week later. She was exhausted and there was something feverish in her eyes. She didn't want to be seen in restaurants or anywhere too busy, but she didn't want to stay home either. When I went to pick her up, I suggested we drive away from the coast, and we ended up on back roads lined with old farm buildings converted into open-air cafés. As we drove, she talked about Enric. She said she had treated him badly: while the poor guy was moldering in prison, she was running around, demanding her right to compete for a place on the Olympic team, but all she'd been doing, in the end, was making a fool of herself. She felt terribly selfish. She said she had always known that Enric was in love with her, but she'd never really thought about it much. He never expressed his emotions; maybe if he'd asked her to sleep with him, things would have worked out differently. She told me she had been staying at a friend's place in Barcelona and at the start she'd been utterly miserable: she cried herself to sleep every night; she had nightmares about the murdered woman; her head ached and her hands shook when visitors came. One day she ran into her old boyfriend in the corridors of the National Sports Institute, and he made a fool of himself. They slept together; she left at midnight convinced she would never see him again. He was asleep and didn't even notice. She didn't mention the meetings or the law suits she was preparing, and I didn't ask. She wanted to visit Enric in prison, and she was looking for someone to go with her. I said I would, but the days went by and Nuria didn't bring it up again. She would turn up at the hotel at the usual time, and we'd go straight up to my room and stay there until it began to get dark. In bed she always talked about the Palacio Benvingut and the old woman. One afternoon, as she was coming, she said I should buy it. I don't have that sort of money, I said. It's a pity, she replied. If you had lots of money we could leave this place forever. I've got enough money for that, I said, but by then she had stopped listening. When we made love she was mostly quiet, but as she approached her climax she'd begin to talk. The problem wasn't so much that Nuria talked while we were having sex, but that she always talked about the same things: murder and skating. As if she was suffocating. The worst thing, though, was that it started to rub off on me, and soon, as our rhythm accelerated, we'd both launch into confessions and gruesome soliloquies full of groans and sheets of ice scattered with old women, and only orgasm could shut us up. How did I feel when I saw the old woman lying in a puddle of blood? Did I know that the blade of a skate was only three millimeters wide and could be a lethal weapon? Why had the old woman gone onto the ice? Was she fleeing from her killer? Did she think the killer wouldn't be able to follow her? Which of them slipped first? Sometimes Nuria went on about Enric. Would he hate her? Was he thinking of her? Was he suicidal? Was he was crazy? Had he killed the old woman? One afternoon she asked me to sodomize her. As I was about to, she said that Enric would have taken it up the ass in prison for sure. Imagining the fat guy, even for an instant, was enough to put me off. One afternoon she told me she had dreamed about the old woman's blood. The blood on the ice formed a letter that nobody had seen, not me or the police or anyone. What letter? A capital N. Another afternoon, instead of getting undressed I suggested we take the car and go see Enric in Gerona. Nuria refused and then began to cry. How could I have been so dumb, she said, why didn't I realize? Realize what? That Enric had built the skating rink without council authorization? No, shouted Nuria, that no one has ever loved me like Enric! He was my true love and I couldn't see it. And she kept coming up with variations on that theme until both of us were exhausted. I soon realized, and I think Nuria did too, that we were heading for a dead end. And yet we had never been so close, or wanted each other so badly . . .

GASPAR HEREDIA:

The police came to the campground twice

The police came to the campground twice, on routine visits, and both times the Peruvian, Miriam from Senegal, Caridad and I pretended to be campers playing pétanque. For such occasions the Peruvian kept various sets of boules in a dog kennel beside the court, and he'd whip around on his bike, if necessary, past the bathrooms and my tent, urgently inviting us to come play. As time went by, we got to like pétanque, and took to playing in the evenings as the sun went down. Our games grew longer and more impassioned. The Peruvian, the receptionist and Miriam made up the day-shift team; while El Carajillo, Caridad and I represented the night-shift. Each team had its pointers, placers or precision players (we never knew what the official term was) and its shooters, knockers or blasters. We usually played under a light, just as it was starting to get dark, sometimes on the road that led into the campground rather than on the courts, or beside the bar, or next to the bathrooms if Miriam still had some cleaning to do. Caridad soon proved to be an outstanding shooter, as did Miriam, while El Carajillo and the Peruvian were born pointers. The receptionist and I just made up the numbers. Alex Bobadilla occasionally replaced the receptionist, with more enthusiasm than skill. In the end we decided to make a selection from our teams and participate in the championship that was held in the campground each year to cap off the season. El Carajillo, the Peruvian and Miriam were selected. The rest of us, including the other two cleaning ladies, who were too busy to play because of their various jobs, were happy to applaud, criticize and drink beer. Around that time, the Peruvian and the receptionist set a date for their wedding, and there was a feeling of confidence and calm in the air, as if everything was going to work out in the end, though everyone knows that nothing ever does. Our team came in third. We won a cup, which Bobadilla and El Carajillo displayed prominently on a shelf in reception. The weather started getting cooler and I began to anticipate the day when my job would come to an end. To be honest I had absolutely no idea what would happen then. Caridad said that living at the campground was like being on vacation. Indefinitely. For me it was like being back at school: I was starting from scratch. We called the tent our house, as a joke I guess, or just to be cute, or maybe because it really was our house. In the morning, when I finished work, we went down to the beach, hopping over the broken slabs of the sidewalk, Caridad still half asleep, both of us wrapped in towels because it was still cool, and then we'd swim and eat and lie in the sun till we fell asleep. We'd wake up at two or three and go back to the campground. The color soon returned to Caridad's cheeks. All the staff, even Rosa and Azucena, grew fond of her, despite their initial misgivings, maybe because she was always ready to give them a hand, cleaning the bathrooms or doing various odd jobs, even helping out at reception during the day so that the Peruvian and the receptionist could go and have a cup of coffee. With the first signs of autumn everyone started making plans, except for us. Miriam was going to look for jobs in private homes; the sisters would be returning to El Prat; the Peruvian hoped to find work in an office or a realty agency as soon as his papers were in order, and El Carajillo would spend another winter shut up in the reception office, keeping watch over the empty campground. When they asked us what our plans were, we didn't know what to say. The plural pronoun embarrassed us. Live in Barcelona, probably, we'd say, throwing each other sidelong glances. Or travel, or go and live in Morocco, or study, or go our separate ways. All we really knew was that we were hanging in a void. But we weren't afraid. Sometimes at night, as I walked through the darker parts of the campground, among empty sites and family-size tents strewn with pine needles, I thought of the skating rink and then I was afraid. Afraid that I might come across something from the rink, snagged, hidden in the darkness. Sometimes the air and the rats scuttling along the branches of the trees almost made that presence visible, and without breaking into a run I'd quickly retrace my steps; I had to hear Caridad's steady breathing on the other side of the yellow tarpaulin that protected our tent before I could calm down and continue on my rounds . . .

ENRIC ROSQUELLES:

Apart from my mother and a few aunts and cousins

Apart from my mother and a few aunts and cousins with
an exemplary sense of solidarity and familial duty, my only
visitors have been Lola and Nuria (who also have an exemplary sense of friendship and solidarity), but their presence meant more to me than a crowd of others. The first to
come was Lola, and I was so surprised and overjoyed to see
her that I burst into tears in the visiting room. Our misun-
derstandings, conflicts and professional disagreements were
forgotten. As soon as I saw her, I knew: it didn't matter
to her that I was a pariah; a true social worker will always
be wherever there is suffering, and there's no doubt about
it, Lola is a social worker through and through. The only
member of my numerous team who never sucked up to me
(I won't deny that I occasionally criticized her in public,
and she infuriated me, and I considered confining her to a
desk job); the only one who dared to visit me when I was in
disgrace. That's the way it is, and it's not too late for me to
learn my lesson: beware the acquiescent, for they will betray
you in the end. I must remember that when I'm released.
Because I will be released, don't you worry. But getting back
to Lola, she came to see me, as cheerful and energetic as
ever, and when I had dried my tears, she said she knew I
couldn't have killed the old woman (who, as it happened,
was one of her—one of our—clients), and the truth, she
was sure, would come out in the end. Things in Z were

terrible: the Social Services Departmewnt was being run by some bootlicker from Fairs and Festivals, who to make things worse was trying to make an impression (though on *whom* remained a mystery) by reorganizing, that is screwing up, my old client services system, as a result of which many of the staff were seriously considering a career move. Some could already sense that Pilar was going to be defeated in the next election, and others resented having been passed over in the restructuring. I suspect that Lola was in the second group, because she also told me that she would soon be moving to a position in the municipality of Gerona, where she would be earning more and would have full control, so they assured her, over her own programs. I felt that the bit about full control was a kind of veiled reproach, since most of our quarrels had begun over programs designed by Lola, which I then changed, adjusted, corrected or simply tossed into the trash, but since her visit I'm willing to accept any kind of reproach from her, veiled or not. Indeed, I'll say it once and for all, Lola was the best of my colleagues, and if, in the wake of my dismissal, she leaves too, I can only fear for the homeless, the kids with problems, and all the people at risk in Z. Of course I wished her the best of luck in her new job and we even joked about what I would do, professionally, when I got out of this hole. The rest of the conversation revolved around my current situation and the hodgepodge of legal and illegal concepts that were being applied to it. A few days later Nuria appeared, and her visit, which I had so often imagined, desired, anticipated and feared, illuminated this wretched cave even more powerfully than Lola's calm friendship. We didn't talk much, both of us were hoarse, but we said what we needed to say to one another. Nuria was much thinner. She was wearing men's clothes, trousers and a black jacket, which hung about her loosely, as if they had belonged to her father. Her eyes were red, which made me think she had been crying before she came. I asked her how she was. Lonely, she said. I spend my nights crying and thinking. Pretty much like me. As she was leaving I noticed that she was wearing men's shoes too: big black shoes, with hard soles and metal plates reinforcing the heels, like skinhead boots. Both Lola and Nuria brought me gifts. Lola's gift was a novel by Remo Morán. Nuria's was the supreme skating book, *Saint Lydwina or the Subtlety of Ice*, by Henri Lefebvre, in French, published by Luna Park in Brussels. For prisoners as for invalids in hospital, there's no better gift than a book. Time is the only thing I have in abundance, although my lawyer assures me I'll soon be free. The murder charge doesn't stand up, so the only charge I'll have to answer is that of embezzlement. To pass the time until the day of my release, I'm reading and trying to reorganize this place a bit. The governor, a career civil servant, who seems slightly confused, perhaps by my presence or by the unfamiliar milieu, has asked me to help him tidy up this pigsty. I've told him he can count on me, I'll help however I can. He is Castilian, single, more or less my age, and I think we understand each other. In a couple of days I wrote up a report on the state of the facility, focusing on sanitation problems and overcrowding, including evaluations, proposals and justifications. A prisoner who works in the library typed it up, and when the governor read it, he congratulated me enthusiastically and suggested that we revise it together, with a view to entering it for a competition organized by the European Prisons Project. It's not a bad idea . . .

Remo Morán:

You can't have a pact with God and the devil at the same time

You can't have a pact with God and the devil at the same time, the Rookie said to me, his eyes brimming with tears. He's forty-eight years old, and life has treated him "worse than a rat." Now that the beaches are almost empty, being there with him is like being in a desert. He's not collecting bottles and cans anymore. He's begging. At some mysterious hour he leaves his desert and wanders from bar to bar in the historic center, asking for a contribution or a little drink, before heading back to the beach where, so he says, he is planning to stay forever. One day he turned up at the hotel, while Alex and I were going over the accounts at a table in the empty restaurant. He looked at us from a distance, with pitiful, imploring eyes, and asked for money. We gave him some. The next day he turned up again, at night, at the door of the restaurant, but this time there were clients: a group of elderly Dutch tourists who were celebrating the end of their vacation. A waiter picked him up by his collar and belt and threw him out, just like in the movies. The Rookie offered no resistance; pathetically compliant, he fell in a heap. I saw it all from behind the bar, where I was washing glasses. Later I told the waiter that was no way to treat people, although the Dutch tourists had been heartily amused. The waiter replied that he was only following Alex's orders. When the party was over, I asked Alex why he had been so hard on a poor beggar who'd done nothing to us. He didn't know, but he distrusted the Rookie instinctively. He didn't like him hanging around the hotel. And he didn't want me seeing him either. What is it you don't like about him, I asked. His eyes, said Alex: they're the eyes of a madman. At night, when I go to the beach, I see him sleeping under the metal frames of the ice cream stands. There's a sweet, rotting smell on the beach, as if inside one of the shacks, closed to the public until next summer, the dead body of a man or a dog had been left among boxes smeared with melted ice cream. We talk, me standing up, him lying on the sand huddled among newspapers and blankets, his face turned to the seawall or hidden by his strange tubular fingers. You must know a better place to sleep, I say. I must know a place, says the Rookie, sobbing . . .

GASPAR HEREDIA:

One night there was a commotion on the terrace of the bar

One night there was a commotion on the terrace of the bar and the waiter came to fetch the night watchmen. El Carajillo, who was half asleep, said I should go first and see what was happening; he'd come if it was serious and I needed backup. It must have been about three in the morning. When I got to the terrace I saw two huge Germans facing each other, separated only by a table strewn with the remains of a meal and broken glass. It seemed they were about to come to blows, and the few spectators sheltering behind trees and cars were anticipating an outbreak of murderous violence. Both Germans were holding empty beer bottles in their right hands, like gangsters in a movie; but although this fight, or at least the insults and threats, had been going on for some time, oddly they hadn't yet broken the bottles, as if brandishing them was threatening enough. As I approached, it became clear that both of them were fairly drunk: their hair was messed up, they were foaming at the mouth, their eyes were bulging and their arm muscles were all clenched. They were already absorbed in the fight awaiting them and supremely indifferent to anything else. They were insulting each other unremittingly; although I couldn't understand a word, the guttural, sarcastic, vicious sounds issuing from their mouths left little room for doubt. Those German words could be heard throughout the campground, against a background of almost perfect silence, marked only by faint, distant-sounding moans of protest from the few campers who were still awake, especially those in tents near the edge of the terrace. The complaints, and for some reason this was disturbing, were as unintelligible as the German insults. The night breeze carried them to me, muted, immaterial and dreamlike, creating, or at least this is how it felt, a kind of dome enclosing the campground and everything in it, whether living or dead. Suddenly, to make things worse, a voice in my head revealed that only one person could break that dome: me. So as I walked across the terrace toward the Germans, knowing that El Carajillo wouldn't come to back me up, and that none of the witnesses present would step in should the Germans decide, as it seemed more and more likely they would, to warm up for the real fight by hammering me, I sensed that something was going to happen (or maybe that's just how it seems to me now, maybe then I was just a bit afraid), that with each step I took toward the gesticulating pair I was taking half a step toward myself. Walking toward the Corsican brothers. Toward the definitive No way, mister. I prepared myself to take a beating and see what would happen next, and in that frame of mind I approached the Germans and told them, in a friendly and not very loud voice, to leave the terrace and go to bed. Then what had to happen happened: the Germans turned their mugs toward me, and from the middle of those mugs, their blue eyes swam like pilot fish through the alcoholic haze and fastened first on me, then on the trunks of the trees that were slowly breaking up the terrace, then on the empty tables, then on the lamps hanging from some of the trailers, and finally, as if discovering the key to the scene, on an indefinite point behind my back. I should say that I too was aware of something behind me, something following me, but I chose not to turn around and look. To tell the truth I was pretty nervous, but after a few moments I noticed a change in the Germans' attitude, as if an inspection of their surroundings had made it instantly clear to them what a serious game it was they were about to play; their eyes retreated into their sockets, moderating the expressive violence that had seemed a natural prelude to blows. One of them, probably the less drunk of the two, stammered out a question. Strange overtones of innocence and purity resonated in his voice. Maybe he asked what the hell was going on. I told them again to go to bed, in English this time. The Germans, however, weren't looking at me, but at something behind my back. For a moment I thought it might be a trap: if I turned around, that pair of brutes would fall on me howling war cries. Curiosity, however, overcame me: I looked over my shoulder. I was so surprised by what I saw that I dropped the flashlight; it broke open on the cement and the batteries (how could there be so many?) went rolling across the terrace and disappeared into the dark. Caridad was behind me, holding a broad kitchen knife, whose blade seemed to be concentrating the sepia glow of the clouds, filtered through the branches above her. Luckily she gave me a wink; otherwise I would have thought she was intending to plant that knife in me. She looked for all the world like a ghost. With a chilling delicacy, she displayed the knife as if displaying one of her breasts. And the Germans must have seen, because now their gazes seemed to be saying, We don't want to die, we don't want to be wounded, we were joking, we don't want anything to do with this. Go to bed, I said, and they did. I watched them walking away through the campground, propping each other up, just a pair of ordinary drunks. When I looked at Caridad again, the knife had disappeared. Gradually, as if emerging from sleep, the campers, who had watched the action from their tents, began to gather in groups, light cigarettes and comment on the performance. Soon they came onto the terrace and offered to buy us drinks. Someone picked up the batteries from my flashlight and gave them to me. Suddenly I found myself drinking wine and eating cockles under the canopy of an enormous tent, like a house, decorated with little paper Catalonian and Andalusian flags. Caridad was beside me, smiling. An old lady was patting me on the arm. Another lady was praising the mettle of Mexicans. It took me a while to realize that she was referring to me. It seemed that no one had seen Caridad's knife except the Germans and myself. Their sudden departure was being credited to my determination to maintain order in the campground. The dropped flashlight: my anger and haste, as I stepped up to whip their asses. Caridad's presence: the understandable concern of a girl in love. The events on the terrace had been obscured by the trees and shadows. Perhaps it was better that way. When we got back to reception, El Carajillo was fast asleep, and we sat outside for a while, quietly enjoying the fresh air, watching a restless, orangey light play on the road: it made the place feel a bit like a submarine. A little while later Caridad said she was going to bed. She got up and I saw her walk through that light back into the campground. Given its size, the knife should have made a visible bulge under her shirt, but I couldn't see anything, and for a moment I thought that the girl with the knife was just a figment of my imagination . . .

ENRIC ROSQUELLES:

The books they gave me

The books they gave me. *Saint Lydwina or the Subtlety of Ice* is an exquisitely illustrated little book about the patron saint of skaters. The story unfolds in the year 1369 and focuses, in a slightly obsessive fashion, on an afternoon that is, so we gather, momentous for the one and only character. Saint Lydwina of Schiedam, who has been immersed in an ocean of doubts for hours, is skating on the frozen surface of a river as the first signs of night begin to appear on the horizon. The frozen river is sometimes described as a "corridor" and sometimes as a "sword" between day and night. The saint, who is young and beautiful, but frowning, skates on in spite of the gathering dusk. In the book we are told that she is going back and forth between two bridges, about five hundred yards apart. Suddenly, the expression on her face changes; her eyes light up and she thinks she understands the ultimate meaning of what she is doing. Just at that point she falls and ("deservedly") breaks a rib. The book ends there, informing us that Saint Lydwina recovered from this accident and returned to skating with, if anything, even greater delight. Remo Morán's novel is entitled *Saint Bernard*, and recounts the deeds of a dog of that breed, or a man named Bernard, later canonized, or a delinquent who goes by that alias. The dog, or the saint, or delinquent, lives in the foothills of a great icy mountain and every Sunday (although in some places it says "every day") he goes around the mountain villages challenging other dogs or men to duels. Gradually, his opponents begin to lose heart, and in the end no one dares to address him. They all apply "the law of ice," to cite the text. Yet Bernard persists and, every Sunday, continues to do the rounds of the villages, challenging the few ill-informed souls who are slow to flee before him. Time passes and Bernard's canine or human opponents grow old and retire from public life, some kill themselves, others die of natural causes, most end up in sad old age homes. As for Bernard, he too grows old, and since he doesn't live in a village, solitude and old age make him tetchy and irascible. The duels continue, of course, and his opponents keep getting younger, although at first he doesn't notice, but then it hits him with the force of a hammer blow. Morán isn't sparing with blood, which pours forth in torrents, or sperm, which spurts abundantly, or tears which rain down on the flimsiest pretexts. Half-way through the novel, Bernard leaves the foothills of the great mountain ("wagging his tail") and spends a season in a valley, and another season following the course of a river. When he returns home, everything continues as before. The duels become more and more violent; his body is gradually covered with scars and roughly stitched wounds. On one occasion he is on the brink of death. On another he is ambushed as he leaves a village. Finally duels are prohibited by decree throughout the land, and Bernard, having repeatedly broken the law, must flee. Then, at the end of the novel, something strange occurs: after shaking off his pursuers, while sheltering in a cave, Bernard undergoes a metamorphosis: his old body splits into two parts, each identical to the original whole. One part rushes down into the valley, shouting with joy. The other climbs laboriously toward the summit of the great mountain, and is never heard of again . . .

Remo Morán:

It kills me to see people leaving like this

It kills me to see people leaving like this, said the Rookie, while I hang on here hoping for a miracle. The elemental miracle or the miracle of understanding. In the afternoon, I'd go down to the beach to see him, and he was almost always in the same place: a stand where a huge guy with a scarred face rented out pedal-boats. The Rookie looked like a dwarf beside him, and felt safe: they didn't talk, they just stayed together until it got dark; then they went off in opposite directions. That was the only pedal-boat stand left on the beach, and there were hardly any takers. To help out, the Rookie sometimes went along the beach offering people pedal-boats, but no one paid any attention. Around that time, Nuria left Z without saying a word to me. According to Laia, she went to live with a friend in Barcelona, where she had found work. Lola and our son moved to Gerona. Alex had started getting ready to close down the jewelry stores, the campground and the hotel (the Cartago would stay open through the winter, as usual) and only emerged from his office for meals. There were very few people left in the campground, except for a group of retired vacationers run wild, who threw a party every night as if they could sense death approaching. The scandal over the Palacio Benvingut had abated, although Rosquelles' embezzlement was still a topic of conversation in Z; the Socialist and Covergencia parties were using it as a political weapon in their battle for the council. Other scandals had come to light throughout Spain, and the world went imperturbably spinning on its way through the void. As for me, I was starting to get tired of Z, and sometimes thought about leaving, but where would I go? I thought about selling up and living on a farm near Gerona, but that was not a good idea. Nor was moving to Barcelona, or returning to Chile. Maybe Mexico, but no, deep down I knew I didn't have the courage to go back there. All we need now is for it to start snowing, said the Rookie one afternoon, as we were walking along the Paseo Marítimo, by the beach, where a few solitary bathers had dug themselves into the sand, or were jogging along in a desperate attempt to lose weight or get into shape. Snowing? Yes, boss, said the Rookie, with a feverish glint in his eye (he was drunk or high), yes, so the snow can cover me up and kill me . . .

GASPAR HEREDIA:

We had a week left to go

We had a week left to go. Bobadilla had started gradually laying off the staff, and one day I woke up and found out that Rosa and Azucena had gone back to El Prat. Before they left, they'd bought a cake and had a little send-off. I was sad to hear they'd gone and sorry to have slept through the party. Caridad saved me a piece of cake, which I ate at the back of the campground, staring at the fences and the shadows moving on the walls of the neighboring buildings, which were almost all empty. The thought of leaving Z filled me with apprehension, but we had to go. In the meantime Caridad suggested we visit the Palacio Benvingut one last time. I flatly refused. Why go back there? It wasn't like we'd left anything behind. It was better to stay within the confines of the campground until the day of our definitive departure. Caridad seemed to be convinced, but she wasn't. For a moment, her eyes were covered by the blurry film that was the sign and agent of a force sucking her away toward another reality. It's because she's exhausted, I told myself, that's all, and her bad diet. Or: when eyes are very dark, black in fact, they're bound look blurry in certain kinds of light. But to be honest I couldn't reassure myself. With each passing day my fear intensified. Fear of what? I can't say for sure, although I guess it was fear of coming to the end of happiness. It's symptomatic of my state of mind that when I was alone, I passed the time making calculations on paper or with a stick on the ground: how much Remo Morán owed me, plus the bonus, and the number of months it would last, roughly until Christmas, a great time to run out of money. I hoped to have another job by then, even if it was playing Santa Claus or one of the Magi. Sometimes I found myself thinking about the police. I dreamed of dim, windswept police stations, and gutted filing cabinets, their contents strewn on the floor, yellow record cards for foreigners whose residency permits had expired years ago, documents that would never be read again, gradually obliterated by time: cases filed and lost. The faces of killers filed and lost. Now the war is over and all legal immigrants are allowed to work. I tried to be positive when I woke up—telling myself the worst was behind us, everything had worked out fine—but I couldn't escape that precarious feeling. Once I was woken by Caridad's voice softly saying that she wanted to go to the Palacio Benvingut to avenge Carmen. I opened my eyes, thinking that she was talking to someone outside the tent, but no, she was lying right beside me, whispering the words into my ear. Why spoil everything with that damn palace? I mumbled, still half asleep. Caridad laughed as if she had been caught playing a mischievous game. Not a glimmer of daylight was showing through the canvas, so I assumed that night had fallen; the silence of the evening in the empty campground was physically chilling, and I had the impression, I don't know why, that there was a dense fog outside. Avenge Carmen? I asked: How? Caridad didn't answer. Do you think the killer will return to the scene of the crime? I felt Caridad's lips moving down from my ear to my neck, where they stopped: I felt her lips, then her teeth, then her tongue. I rolled over, feeling sick, and tried to make out her face. Caridad's eyes were invisible in the darkness. Poor Carmen, she said, I know who killed her. I've talked about it with your friend Remo. When? I asked. He came to see me a couple days ago and we had a good talk about it. So Remo knows who killed Carmen? Me too, said Caridad. Why do you want to go to the Palacio Benvingut, then? You should go to the police, I said. After that, there was no way I could get back to sleep . . .

Enric Rosquelles:

I was released a week after

I was released a week after my essay won first prize in the European Prison Project competition, sponsored by the EU. The time spent in prison had, I felt, calmed my nerves and allowed me to adopt a more detached and balanced outlook. Definitely more detached and balanced. Some prisoners say it's pretty much the same inside and outside. And they're not entirely wrong. But personally I prefer life on the outside. I had lost weight and grown a moustache; I was also, surprising as it may seem, much more suntanned than before, and in perfect health. At the gate I was met by my mother and aunts, and before I knew what was going on, I was at the home of one of my cousins (the architect), where I remained hidden for three days, under the control of my mother's family; that much at least was due to them, they felt, given their contribution to the bail. In private, my cousin's wife confessed to me that they'd feared another act of madness on my part. Suicide! The poor dears! If I hadn't killed myself inside, why would I try now that I was free, with my family to support me? But I didn't contradict them; I let them organize my life however they liked. In any case, I have always respected the family's solid good sense. During this new confinement, my contact with the outside world was limited to a few phone calls. I spoke with the governor of the Gerona prison, who was not only delighted about the prize but had already started planning further articles for us to write together, on a range of what he called "sociological" topics. Juanito, that was his name, was thinking of asking for a year's leave of absence from the civil service, because, as a result of the prize, he had been offered a job by an important publishing house in Madrid, and as he said, Why not give it a try? I can't remember if the publishing house specialized in "sociological" books or literature, but whichever it was, I'm sure Juanito will go far. I made another call, trying to find Nuria. First I spoke with her mother, then with Laia. Her mother informed me, in a polite but cool tone, that Nuria no longer lived in Z, and as far as she knew, her daughter would prefer not to see me again. Later I spoke with Laia, who told me that Nuria was working as a secretary for a Dutch firm with an office in Barcelona, and that a month or so earlier photos of her had appeared in a well-known magazine with a nationwide circulation. What photos? Artistic nude shots, said Laia, controlling the urge to laugh. I spent more than a week trying to get hold of the magazine, but all my efforts were in vain. One night, when I was back home, I dreamed I was searching for the nude shots of Nuria, wandering in pajamas through a vast dusty newspaper archive, which resembled (and just remembering this gives me goose bumps) the Palacio Benvingut. Coated in grey gelatin, suffocating in silence, I rummaged on shelves and in boxes, with the dim certitude that if I could find the photos, I would understand the significance, the cause, the true and hidden meaning of what had happened to me. But the photos never turned up . . .

Remo Morán:

I killed her, boss, said the Rookie

I killed her, boss, said the Rookie, as the waves washed up the sand toward his knees, at regular intervals, each coming a little closer than the last. The beach was empty; on the horizon, over the sea, fat black clouds were stirring. In an hour, I thought, the first storm of autumn would pass over Z like an aircraft carrier, and no one would hear us. (No one would hear us?) Don't ask me why, boss, said the Rookie, I swear I don't even know myself, though it's probably because I'm sick. But what's wrong with me? I don't feel any pain. What demon or devil possessed me? Is it because of this miserable town? The Rookie was kneeling on the sand, looking out to sea with his back to me, so I couldn't see his face, but I thought he was crying. His hair was sticking to his skull; it looked like it was slicked down with gel. I told him to calm down; we could go somewhere else. (Where was I going to take him?) I didn't leave when I should have left, he replied, which proves that I still have balls, and I've waited as long as humanly possible for the truth to dawn on the police, but nobody wants to work in this country, so here I am, boss, he sighed. At last the waves reached the Rookie's knees. A shiver ran through his ragged clothes. I took the knife she kept to defend herself (who from? not me!) and from that moment on I was a wild animal, sobbed the Rookie. What are they waiting for? Why don't they arrest me? Why would they arrest you when you're not even a suspect? I said. The Rookie kept quiet for a moment; the storm was already overhead. I killed her, boss, that's a fact, and now this crazy, miserable town seems have gone on honeymoon. It began to pour. Before getting up and heading back to the hotel, I asked him how he had known that the singer lived in the Palacio Benvingut. The Rookie turned and looked at me with the innocence of a child (between two flashes of lightning I saw the freshly washed face of my son, dripping with water): By following her, boss, following her up and down these hilly streets, just trying to keep watch over her. Just looking for a little human warmth. Was she alone? The Rookie drew signs in the air. There's nothing more to say, he said . . .

GASPAR HEREDIA:

We took the Barcelona train one overcast afternoon

We took the Barcelona train one overcast afternoon, after a rainy morning that flooded the few tents still pitched at Stella Maris. Our belongings turned out to be more numerous than a quick inspection had led us to believe, so we needed some plastic bags, which we found at the only supermarket still open. Even so we had no choice but to abandon quite a few things that Caridad was attached to: magazines, press cuttings, seashells, stones, an ample range of souvenirs of Z. I hope that when Bobadilla finds those remains he slings them in the trash without a second thought. The night before we left, Remo came to the office and handed me an envelope with my pay and a substantial bonus: enough to buy one-way tickets to Mexico for Caridad and me. Remo and I talked for a while on the far side of the pool, where no one could hear us. I suspect we were both hiding something. It was a brief farewell: I accompanied him to the gate, and thanked him. Morán told me to take care; we hugged and off he went. I have never seen him since. That night Caridad and I said goodbye to El Carajillo. The next morning was hectic: the rain leaked into the tent and wet our clothes and sleeping bags. We were soaking when we left for the station. By the time we got there it had stopped raining. On the other side of the tracks, in an orchard, I saw a donkey. He was under a tree, and every now and then he brayed, making all the travelers on the platforms turn to look at him. He seemed to be happy, after the rain. Then, as if spewed from a black cloud, two cops from the national police and a *guardia civil* appeared at the end of the station. I thought they had come to arrest us. From the corner of my eye, I watched them walk along toward us, in no hurry at all, gun hands at the ready. We're two of a kind, that donkey and me, said Caridad in a dreamy voice. Foreigners in our own land. I would have liked to tell her she was wrong, to point out that in the eyes of the law, I was the only foreigner, but I kept my mouth shut. I put my arm gently around her waist and waited. Caridad might have been foreign to God, to the police and even to herself, but she wasn't foreign to me. I could have said the same for the donkey. The cops stopped halfway down the platform. They went into the station bar, first the police, then the *guardia civil*, and by an auditory miracle I clearly heard them order two coffees with milk and one *carajillo*. The donkey brayed again. We kept watching him for a good while. Caridad put her arm around my shoulders and we stayed like that until the train came . . .

ENRIC ROSQUELLES:

When I finally returned to Z, it was all so different

When I finally returned to Z, it was all so different that my first thought was: I must have taken a wrong turn. For a start, no one recognized me, which was amazing, given that for several weeks I had been the talk of the town, and it was hard to believe that the whole business had been forgotten so quickly. Secondly, many of the buildings and streets in Z looked unfamiliar, as if the townscape had been modified in subtle but distressingly noticeable ways: the storefronts seemed to be elements in a vast camouflage operation; the bare trees were not where they should have been, and in some streets the flow of the traffic had altered substantially. But as I got out of the car, I noticed that City Hall presented the same imperturbable façade, although Pilar was no longer mayor (she had been easily beaten in the last election) and I was no longer her trusty factotum. I came to the bittersweet understanding that the institution would remain the same in spite of changing circumstances, or to put it another way: even though human beings like Pilar and myself were prepared to give our all and sacrifice our careers in the attempt to bring about change, nothing could shift the venerable and senseless stones of City Hall. Having realized that, it was easier to accept the transformation of the town. In any case, applying the principle of caution, which I had recently come to appreciate in prison, all I did was have a drink in a bar and use the washroom, then walk along the Paseo Marítimo to stretch my legs a bit, before going back to the car. Was I tempted to visit the Palacio Benvingut? Well, the simplest answer would be no, or yes. To tell the truth, I did drive out that way, but that's all. There's a curve in the highway on the way to Y, from which you can see the cove and the palace. When I got there I braked, turned around and drove back to Z. What good would it have done me, going there? I would only have been adding to the sum of pain. Besides, in winter, it's a sad place. The stones I remembered as blue were grey. The paths I remembered as bathed in light were strewn with shadows. So I braked, made a U-turn and drove back to Z. I avoided looking in the rearview mirror until I was a safe distance away. What's gone is gone, that's what I say, you have to keep looking ahead . . .